DEATH AND A DOG

DEATH AND A DOG

(A Lacey Doyle Cozy Mystery—Book 2)

FIONA GRACE

FIONA GRACE

Debut author Fiona Grace is author of the LACEY DOYLE COZY MYSTERY series which includes MURDER IN THE MANOR (Book #1), DEATH AND A DOG (Book #2) and CRIME IN THE CAFE (Book #3). Fiona would love to hear from you, so please visit www.fionagraceauthor.com to receive free ebooks, hear the latest news, and stay in touch.

TABLE OF CONTENTS

CHAPTER ONE

The bell above the door tinkled. Lacey looked up and saw an elderly gentleman had wandered into her antiques store. He was dressed in English countryman attire, which would've looked peculiar in Lacey's old home, New York City, but here in the seaside town of Wilfordshire, England, he was just another one of the locals. Only, Lacey didn't recognize him as she now did most of the small town's residents. His bemused expression made her wonder if he was lost.

Realizing he may need some help, she quickly covered the mouthpiece of the telephone she was holding—mid-conversation with the RSPCA—and called over the counter to him, "I'll be with you in just a second. I just need to finish up this call."

The man didn't seem to hear her. His focus was fixed on a shelf filled with frosted crystal figurines.

Lacey knew she'd have to hurry her conversation with the RSPCA along so she could attend to the confused-looking customer, so she removed her hand from the mouthpiece. "Sorry about that. Could you repeat what were you saying?"

The voice on the other end was male, and he sounded weary as he sighed. "What I was saying, Miss Doyle, is that I cannot give out details of staff members. It's for security reasons. Surely you get that?"

Lacey had heard this all before. She'd first called the RSPCA to officially adopt Chester, the English Shepherd dog who had more or less come with the antiques store she was leasing (his prior owners, who'd leased the store before her, had died in a tragic accident, and Chester had wandered all the way back to his home). But she'd gotten the shock of her life when the woman on the other end of the line had asked her if she was related to Frank Doyle—the father who'd abandoned her at the age of seven. Their call had gotten disconnected,

I

and she'd rung back every day since to trace the woman she'd spoken to. But it turned out all calls now went to a central call center located in the closest city of Exeter, and Lacey could never track down the woman who'd somehow known her father by name.

Lacey tightened her grip on the receiver and fought to keep her voice steady. "Yes, I understand you can't tell me her name. But aren't you able to *transfer* me to her?"

"No, ma'am," the young man replied. "Beyond the fact I don't know who this woman is, we have a *call center system*. The calls are randomly allocated. All I can do—and have done already—is put a notice on our system with your details." He was starting to sound exasperated.

"But what if she doesn't see the notice?"

"That's a very real possibility. We have tons of staff members who work voluntarily on an ad hoc basis. The person you spoke with before might not have even been into the office since the original call."

Lacey had heard these words before, too, from the numerous calls she'd made, but each time she wished and prayed for a different outcome. The call center staff seemed to be getting pretty irritated with her.

"But if she was a volunteer, doesn't that mean she might never be back for another shift?" Lacey asked.

"Sure. There's a chance. But I don't know what you want me to do about it."

Lacey had had enough of cajoling for the day. She sighed and admitted defeat. "Okay, well thank you anyway."

She put down the phone, her chest sinking. But she wasn't going to dwell on it. Her attempts to find information about her father seemed to be two steps forward, one and a half back, and she was getting used to the dead ends and disappointments. Besides, she had a customer to see to, and her beloved store always took precedence in Lacey's mind above all else.

Ever since the two police detectives, Karl Turner and Beth Lewis, had posted their official notice to say she'd had nothing to do with the murder of Iris Archer—and that she had, indeed, helped them solve the case—Lacey's store had bounced right back. Now it was flourishing, with a steady stream of daily customers made up of locals and tourists. Lacey had enough of an income now to buy Crag Cottage (something she was in the process of negotiating with Ivan Parry, her current landlord), and she even had enough income to pay Gina, her next door neighbor and close friend, for semi-permanent working hours. Not that Lacey took the time during Gina's shift off—she used it to study up on auctioneering. She'd enjoyed the one she'd conducted for Iris Archer's belongings so much, she was going to hold one every month. Tomorrow, Lacey's next auction was to commence, and she was buzzing with excitement for it.

She went out from behind the counter—Chester raising his head to give her his customary whinny—and approached the elderly man. He was a stranger, not one of her regular customers, and was peering intently at the display shelf of crystal ballerinas.

Lacey pushed her dark curls off her face and came out from behind the counter, heading toward the elderly man.

"Are you looking for anything in particular?" she asked as she drew up beside him.

The man jumped. "Goodness, you frightened me!"

"I'm so sorry," Lacey said, noticing his hearing aid for the first time and reminding herself not to sneak up behind old people in the future. "I just wondered if you were looking for anything specific, or if you were just perusing?"

The man looked back to the figures, a small smile on his lips. "It's a funny story," he said. "It's my late wife's birthday. I came to town for some tea and cake, as a sort of remembrance celebration, you see. But as I passed your store, I felt the urge to come in." He pointed at the figurines. "First thing I saw were these." He gave Lacey a knowing smile. "My wife was a dancer."

Lacey returned the smile, touched by the poignancy of the story. "How lovely!"

"It was back in the seventies," the elderly man continued, reaching out a shaking hand and taking a model off the shelf. "She was with the Royal Ballet Society. In fact, she was their first ever ballerina with—"

Just then, the sound of a large van careening too fast over the speed bump directly outside the store cut off the end of the man's sentence. The subsequent *bang* it made as it jolted down onto the other side of the bump made him jump a mile, and the figurine went flying from his hands. It hit the wooden floorboards. The ballerina's arm snapped right off and went skittering away under the shelving unit.

"Oh my goodness!" the man exclaimed. "I'm so sorry!"

"Don't worry," Lacey assured him, her gaze fixed out the window at the white van, which had pulled up to the curb and drawn to a halt, its engine now idling and belching smoke from the exhaust pipe. "It wasn't your fault. I don't think the driver saw the bump. He's probably damaged his van!"

She crouched down and reached with an arm beneath the shelving unit, until her fingertips brushed against the little jagged edge of crystal. She pulled the arm out—which was now covered in a fine layer of dust—and drew herself back up to standing, just as she saw through the window the driver of the van hopping down from the cabin to the cobblestones.

"You have *got* to be kidding me . . ." Lacey muttered, narrowing her eyes at the culprit she could now identify. "Taryn."

Taryn owned the boutique store next door. She was a snobbish, petty woman, whom Lacey had awarded the title of Least Favorite Person in Wilfordshire. She was always trying to mess with Lacey, to drive her out of town. Taryn had done everything in her power to frustrate Lacey's attempts to start a business here in Wilfordshire, all the way down to drilling holes in her own store wall just to irritate her! And though the woman had asked for a truce after her handyman had taken things a little too far and been caught loitering outside Lacey's cottage one night, Lacey hadn't been so confident she could trust her again. Taryn played dirty. This was surely another one of her tricks. For starters, there was no way she didn't know the speed bump was there—it was visible from her own store's window, for goodness sake! So she'd driven over it too fast deliberately. Then to add insult to injury, she'd parked it right in front of *Lacey's* store, rather than her own, either in an attempt to block the view, or in order to pump fumes in her direction.

"I'm so sorry," the man repeated, pulling Lacey's attention back to the moment. He was still holding up the figurine, now one-armed. "Please. Let me pay for the damage."

"Absolutely not," Lacey told him firmly. "You did nothing wrong." Her narrow-eyed gaze roved back over his shoulder and out the window. She fixed it on Taryn, following the woman as she gingerly waltzed to the back of the van like she had no cares in the world. Lacey's annoyance at the boutique owner grew stronger. "If anyone's to blame, it's the driver." She tightened her hands into fists. "It's almost as if they did it deliberately. Ow!"

Lacey felt something sharp in her palm. She'd squeezed the broken ballerina's arm so tightly, it had nicked her skin.

"Oh!" the man exclaimed at the sight of the bright globule of blood swelling in her palm. He pincer-gripped the offending arm from the middle of her hand, as if removing it might somehow mend the wound. "Are you okay?"

"Please excuse me for one second," Lacey said.

She headed for the door—leaving the bemused-looking man behind in her store holding a broken ballerina in one hand and a disembodied arm in the other—and marched onto the street. She paced right up to her neighborhood nemesis.

"Lacey!" Taryn beamed, as she heaved up the back door of the van. "Hope you don't mind me parking here? I have the new season's stock to unload. Isn't summer just your favorite season for fashion?"

"I don't mind you parking there at all," Lacey said. "But I do mind you driving too fast over the speed bump. You know the bump is right in front of my store. The noise almost gave my customer a heart attack."

She noted then, that Taryn had also parked in such a manner that her bulky van blocked Lacey's view across the street to Tom's patisserie. *That* was definitely purposeful!

"Got it," Taryn said with fake joviality. "I'll make sure to drive slower when it's time to get in the autumn season's stock. Hey, you should pop in once I've set all this up. Switched up your wardrobe. Treat yourself. You deserve it." Her eyes roved down Lacey's outfit. "And it's certainly time."

"I'll think about it," Lacey said tonelessly, matching Taryn's fake smile with her own.

The second she turned her back on the woman, her smile turned into a grimace. Taryn really was the queen of the back-handed compliment.

When she got back into her store, Lacey discovered her elderly customer was now waiting by the counter, and a second person—a man in a dark suit—had also entered. He was perusing the shelf filled with all the nautical items Lacey was planning on auctioning tomorrow, while under the watchful eye of Chester the dog. She could smell his aftershave even from this distance.

"I'll be with you in a moment," Lacey called over to the new customer as she hurried toward the back of the store where the elderly gentleman was waiting.

"Is your hand okay?" the man asked her.

"Absolutely fine." She looked down at the small scratch in her palm, which had already stopped bleeding. "Sorry for rushing off like that. I had to—" she chose her words carefully, "—*attend* to something."

Lacey was determined not to let Taryn get her down. If she let the boutique owner get under her skin, it would be akin to scoring an own goal.

As Lacey slid behind the sales counter, she noticed the elderly gentleman had placed the broken figurine upon it.

"I'd like to buy it," he announced.

"But it's broken," Lacey countered. He was obviously just trying to be nice, even though he had no reason to feel bad about the breakage. It really hadn't been his fault at all.

"I still want it."

Lacey blushed. He really was adamant.

"Can you let me try to fix it first, at least?" she said. "I have some super glue and—"

"Not at all!" the man interrupted. "I want it just as it is. You see, it reminds me of my wife even more now. That's what I was just about to say, when the van went bump. She was the Royal Ballet Society's first ballerina with a disability." He held up the figure, twirling it in the light. Light caught off the right arm, which still looked elegant outstretched despite stopping in a jagged stump at the elbow. "She danced with one arm."

Lacey's eyebrows rose. Her mouth fell open. "No way!"

The man nodded eagerly. "Honest! Don't you see? This was a sign from her."

Lacey couldn't help but agree. She was searching for her own ghost, after all, in the form of her father, so she was particularly sensitive to the signs of the universe.

"Then you're right, you have to take it," Lacey said. "But I can't charge you for it."

"Are you sure?" the man asked, surprised.

Lacey beamed. "I'm positive! Your wife sent you a sign. The figurine is rightfully yours."

The man looked touched. "Thank you."

Lacey began to wrap the figurine up in tissue paper for him. "Let's make sure she doesn't lose any more of her limbs, huh?"

"You're holding an auction, I see," the man said, pointing over her shoulder at the poster hanging on the wall.

Unlike the crude hand-drawn posters that had advertised her last auction, Lacey had had this one professionally made. It was decorated with nautical imagery; boats and seagulls, and a border made to look like blue and white gingham bunting in honor of Wilfordshire's own bunting obsession.

"That's right," Lacey said, feeling a swell of pride in her chest. "It's my second auction ever. It's exclusively for antique navy items. Sextants. Anchors. Telescopes. I'll be selling a whole array of treasures. Perhaps you'd like to attend?"

"Perhaps I will," the man replied with a smile.

"I'll put a flier in the bag for you."

Lacey did just that, then handed the man his precious figurine across the counter. He thanked her and headed away.

Lacey watched the elderly man exit the store, touched by the story he'd shared with her, before remembering that she had another customer to attend to.

She looked right to turn her attention to the other man. Only now she saw he had gone. He'd slipped out silently, unnoticed, before she'd even had a chance to see whether he needed any help.

She went over to the area he'd been perusing—the bottom shelf where she'd placed storage boxes filled with all the items she was selling at the auction tomorrow. A sign, in Gina's handwriting, stated: *None of this lot is for general sale. Everything will be auctioned!* She'd doodled what appeared to be a skull and cross-bones beneath, evidently confusing the Navy theme with a pirate one. Hopefully the customer had seen the sign and would be back tomorrow to bid on whatever item it was he was so interested in.

Lacey took one of the boxes filled with items she'd not yet valued out, and carried it back to the desk. As she took out item after item, lining them up on the counter, she couldn't help feeling excitement coursing through her. Her last auction had been wonderful, yet tempered by the fact she was hunting for a killer. This one, she'd be able to fully enjoy. She'd really get a chance to flex her auctioneers muscles, and she literally couldn't wait!

She'd just gotten into the flow of valuing and cataloguing the items when she was interrupted by the shrill sound of her cell phone. A little frustrated to be disturbed by what was undoubtedly her melodramatic younger sister, Naomi, with a single-parent-related crisis, Lacey glanced over at the cell where it lay face up on the counter. To her surprise, the ID flashing up at her was *David*, her recently ex-husband.

Lacey stared at the flashing screen for a moment, stunned into inaction. A tsunami of different emotions rushed through her. She and David had exchanged precisely zero words with one another since the divorce—although he seemed to still be on speaking terms with Lacey's *mother* of all people—and had dealt with everything through their solicitors. But for him to be calling her directly? Lacey didn't even know where to begin theorizing why he'd be doing such a thing.

Against her better judgment, Lacey answered the call.

"David? Is everything okay?"

"No, it's not," came his sharp-sounding voice, bringing forth about a million latent memories that had been lying dormant in Lacey's mind, like dust stirred.

She tensed, preparing for some terrible bombshell. "What is it? What happened?"

"Your alimony didn't come through."

Lacey rolled her eyes so hard they hurt. Money. Of course. There was nothing that mattered more to David than money. One of the most ludicrous aspects of her divorce from David was the fact that she had to pay him spousal support because she'd been the higher earner of the pair. It figured that the only thing to compel him to make actual contact with her would be *that*.

"But I set the payment up through the bank," Lacey told him. "It should be automatic."

"Well, evidently the Brits have a different interpretation of the word automatic," he said haughtily. "Because no money has been deposited in my bank account, and if you weren't aware, the deadline is today! So I suggest you get on the phone to your bank immediately and resolve the situation."

He sounded just like a headmaster. Lacey half-expected him to finish his monologue with the phrase, "you silly little girl."

She squeezed the cell phone, tightly, trying her hardest not to let David get to her, not today, the day before her auction that she was so looking forward to!

"What a clever suggestion, David," she replied, wedging the phone between her ear and shoulder so she could free her hands and use them to log onto her online bank account. "I'd never have thought to do that myself."

Her words were met by silence. David had probably never heard her use sarcasm before, and it had thrown him. She blamed Tom for that. Her new beau's English sense of humor was rubbing off on her very quickly.

"You're not taking this very seriously," David replied, once he'd finally caught up.

"Should I be?" Lacey replied. "It's just a mix-up at the bank. I can probably get it taken care of by the end of the day. In fact, yes, there's a notice here on my account." She clicked on the little red icon and an information box popped up. She read it aloud. "*Due to the bank holiday, any scheduled payment dates that fall on either Sunday or Monday will reach accounts on Tuesday.*' Aha. There you go. I knew it would be something simple. A bank holiday." She paused and looked out the window at the throng of passing people. "I did think the streets looked extra busy today."

She could practically hear David grinding his teeth through the speaker.

"It's actually extremely inconvenient," he snapped. "I do have bills to pay, you know."

Lacey looked over at Chester, as if in need of a comrade in this particularly frustrating conversation. He raised his head off his paws and quirked up an eyebrow.

"Can't Frida lend you a couple million bucks if you're short?"

"Eda," David corrected.

Lacey knew full well the name of David's new fiancée. But she and Naomi had taken to calling her Fortnight Frida, in reference to the speed with which the two had gotten engaged and now she couldn't think of her as anything else.

"And no," he continued. "She shouldn't have to. Who even told you about Eda?"

"My mother might have let it slip on one or two dozen occasions. What are you doing talking to my mom anyway?"

"She'd been a part of my family for fourteen years. I didn't divorce *her.*"

Lacey sighed. "No. I guess not. So what's the plan? The three of you go and bond over a mani-pedi?"

Now she was trying to wind him up, and she couldn't help herself. It was quite fun.

"You're being ridiculous," David said.

"Isn't she the heiress to a false nail emporium?" she said with feigned innocence.

"Yes, but you don't have to say it like that," David said, in a voice that catapulted the image of his pout-face right into Lacey's mind's eye.

"I was just speculating on how the three of you will likely spend your time together."

"With a tone of criticism."

"Mom tells me she's young," Lacey said, changing course. "Twenty. I mean, I think twenty might be a little too young for a man your age, but at least she's got a full nineteen years to work out whether she wants children or not. Thirty-nine is the cut-off point for you, after all."

No sooner had she said it than she realized just how much like Taryn she sounded. She shuddered. While she had no qualms over Tom's mannerisms rubbing off on her, she most certainly drew the line at Taryn's!

"Sorry," she mumbled, back-tracking. "That was uncalled for."

David let a beat pass. "Just get me my money, Lace."

The call went dead.

Lacey sighed and put the phone down. As infuriating as the conversation had been, she was absolutely determined not to let it bring her down. David was in her past now. She'd built a whole new life for herself here in Wilfordshire. And anyway, David moving on with Eda was a blessing in disguise. She wouldn't have to pay him alimony anymore once they married, and the problem would be solved! But knowing the way things usually went for her, she had the feeling it would be a very long engagement.

CHAPTER TWO

Lacey was in the middle of her valuing work when, out the window, Taryn finally moved her huge van, and the view to Tom's store across the cobblestone streets opened up. The gingham Easter-themed bunting had been replaced with summer-themed bunting, and Tom had upgraded his macaron display so that it now depicted a tropical island scene. Lemon macarons made up the sand, surrounded by a sea of different blues—turquoise (cotton candy flavor), baby blue (bubblegum flavor), dark blue (blueberry flavor) and navy blue (blue raspberry flavor). Tall stacks of chocolate macarons, coffee macarons, and peanut macarons formed the bark of palm trees, and the leaves had been constructed out of marzipan; another food-based material Tom was proficient at working with. The window display was awe-inspiring, not to mention mouth-watering, and it always drew a huge crowd of excited tourist spectators.

Looking through the window to the counter, Lacey could see Tom behind it, busy delighting his customers with his theatrical displays.

She sank her chin onto her fist and let out a dreamy sigh. So far, things with Tom had been going wonderfully. They were officially "dating," which was Tom's choice of word, not hers. During their "defining the relationship" discussion, Lacey had put forth the argument that it was an inadequate and childish term for two full-grown adults embarking on a romantic journey together, but Tom pointed out that since she wasn't employed by Merriam-Webster, the terminology wasn't really hers to decide. She'd conceded on that particular point, but drew the line at the terms 'girlfriend' and 'boyfriend'. They were yet to decide on the appropriate terms to refer to one another and usually defaulted to 'dear'.

Suddenly, Tom was looking at her and waving. Lacey jerked up, her cheeks warming at the realization he'd just caught her gazing at him like a schoolgirl with a crush.

Tom's waving gesture turned into a beckoning, and Lacey suddenly realized what the time was. Ten past eleven. Tea time! And she was ten minutes late for their daily Elevenses!

"Come on, Chester," she said quickly, as excitement leapt into her breast. "It's time to visit Tom."

She practically ran out of the store, only just remembering to flip her 'Open' sign over so it read *back in 10 minutes* and lock the door. Then she hop-skipped across the cobblestone street toward the patisserie, her heart beat *thump-thump-thumping* in time with her bouncy steps, as her excitement at seeing Tom ratcheted up.

Just as Lacey reached the door of the patisserie, the group of Chinese vacationers Tom had been entertaining moments earlier came streaming out. Each was clutching an extremely large brown paper bag stuffed full of delicious-smelling goodies, chattering and giggling to each other. Lacey held the door patiently, waiting for them to file past, and they politely bowed their heads in thanks.

Once the path was finally clear, Lacey went inside.

"Hello, my dear," Tom said, a large grin lighting up his handsome, golden-hued face, making laugh lines appear beside his twinkling green eyes.

"I see your groupies just left," Lacey joked, coming toward the counter. "And they bought a ton of merchandise."

"You know me," Tom replied, with an eyebrow wiggle. "I'm the world's first pastry chef with a fan club."

He seemed to be in a particularly jovial mood today, Lacey thought, not that he ever seemed anything but sunny. Tom was one of those people who seemed to breeze through life unperturbed by the usual stresses that got the best of us down. It was one of the things Lacey adored about him. He was so different from David, who would get stressed by the smallest of irritants.

She reached the counter and Tom stretched up on his arms to kiss her over it. Lacey let herself get lost in the moment, only breaking apart when Chester began to whine his displeasure at being ignored.

"Sorry, buddy," Tom said. He came out from behind the counter and offered Chester a chocolate-free carob treat. "There you go. Your favorite."

Chester licked the treats right out of Tom's hand, then let out a long sigh of satisfaction and sank down to the floor for a snooze.

"So, what tea is on the menu today?" Lacey asked, taking her usual stool at the counter.

"Chicory," Tom said.

He headed into the kitchen at the back.

"I haven't had that before," Lacey called out.

"It's caffeine free," Tom called back, over the whoosh of a faucet and the banging of cupboard doors. "And has a slight laxative effect if you drink too much."

Lacey laughed. "Thanks for the heads-up," she called.

Her words were met by the clink and clatter of chinaware, and the bubble of the kettle boiling.

Then Tom reappeared holding a tea tray. Plates, cups, saucers, a sugar bowl, and a china teapot were on it.

He placed the tray down between them. Like all of Tom's crockery, the items were completely mismatched, their only linking theme being Britain, as if he'd sourced each one from a different patriotic old lady's yard sale. Lacey's cup had a photograph of the late Princess Diana on it. Her plate had a passage from Beatrix Potter written in delicate cursive beside a watercolor image of the iconic Aylesbury duck, Jemima Puddleduck, in her bonnet and shawl. The teapot was in the shape of a gaudily decorated Indian elephant, with the words *Piccadilly Circus* printed on its bright red and gold saddle. Its trunk, naturally, made the spout.

As the tea brewed in the pot, Tom used silver tongs to select some croissants from the counter display, which he placed on pretty floral plates. He slid Lacey's toward her, followed by a pot of her favorite apricot jam. Then he poured them both a mug of the now brewed tea, sat in his stool, held up the mug, and said, "Cheers."

With a smile, Lacey clinked hers against his. "Cheers."

As they sipped in unison, Lacey had a sudden flash of déjà vu. Not a real one, like when you're certain you've lived this exact moment before, but the déjà vu that comes from repetition, from routine, from doing the same thing day in day out. It felt like they had done this before, because they had; yesterday, and the day before that, and the day before that. As busy shop owners, Lacey and Tom often put in overtime and worked seven-day weeks. It had come so naturally, the routine, the rhythm. But it was more than that. Tom had automatically given her her favorite toasted almond croissant with apricot jam. He didn't even need to ask what she wanted.

It should have pleased Lacey, but instead, it perturbed her. Because that's exactly how things had been with David to begin with. Learning each other's orders. Doing little favors for one another. Small moments of routine and rhythm that made her feel like they were puzzle pieces that fit perfectly together. She'd been young and foolish and had made the mistake of thinking it would always feel that way. But it had just been the honeymoon period. It wore off a year or two down the line, and by that point, she was already stuck in marriage.

Was that all this relationship was with Tom? A honeymoon period that would eventually wear off?

"What are you thinking?" Tom asked, his voice intruding on her anxious rumination.

Lacey almost spat out her tea. "Nothing."

Tom raised a single eyebrow. "Nothing? The chicory has had such little impact on you all thoughts have vacated your mind?"

"Oh, about the chicory!" she exclaimed, blushing.

Tom looked even more amused. "Yes. What else would I be asking?"

Lacey clumsily placed the Diana cup back on the saucer, making a loud clatter. "It's nice. Licorice-y. Eight out of ten."

Tom whistled. "Wow. High praise. But not quite enough to dethrone the Assam."

"It will take an exceptional tea to dethrone the Assam."

Her momentary panic that Tom had mind-reading abilities subsided, and Lacey turned her attention to the breakfast, savoring the flavors of homemade apricot jam combined with toasted almonds and yummy buttery pastry. But even the tasty food couldn't keep her mind from wandering to the conversation with David. It had been the first time she'd heard his voice since he'd stormed out of their old Upper East Side apartment with the parting declaration, "You'll be hearing from my lawyer!" and something about hearing his voice again reminded her that less than a month ago she'd been a relatively happily married woman, with a stable job and an income and family nearby in the city she'd lived her whole life. Without even knowing she was doing it, she'd blocked out her past life in New York City with a solid wall in her mind. It was a coping strategy she'd developed as a child to cope with the grief of her father's sudden disappearance. Evidently, hearing David's voice had shaken the foundations of that wall.

"We should go on a vacation," Tom suddenly said.

Once again, Lacey almost spit out her food, but Tom couldn't have noticed, because he kept speaking.

"When I'm back from my focaccia course, we should go on a stay-cation. We've both been working so hard, we deserve it. We can go to my hometown in Devon, and I'll show you all the places I loved as a child."

Had Tom suggested this yesterday *before* her call with David, Lacey probably would've bitten his hand off at the offer. But suddenly the idea of making long-term plans with her new beau—even if it was only one *week* in the future—seemed to be jumping the gun. Of course, Tom had no reason not to be confident with his life. But Lacey herself had not been long divorced. She'd entered into his world of relative stability at a point when literally *every* bit of hers had become unmoored—from her job, to her home, to her country, and even her relationship status! She'd gone from babysitting her nephew, Frankie, while her sister, Naomi, went on yet another disastrous date, to shooing sheep off her front lawn; from being barked at by her boss, Saskia, in a New York City interior design firm, to antique-scouting trips in London's Mayfair with her peculiar cardigan-clad neighbor and two sheep dogs in tow. It was a lot of change all in one go, and she wasn't entirely sure where her head was at.

"I'll have to see how busy I am with the store," she replied noncommittally. "The auction is taking more work than I anticipated."

"Sure," Tom said, sounding in no way like he'd read between the lines. Picking up on subtleties and subtext was not one of Tom's fortes, which was another thing she liked about him. He took everything she said on face value. Unlike her mom and sister, who'd needle and prod her and dissect every word she said, there was no guessing or second-guessing with Tom. What you saw was what you got.

Just then, the bell above the patisserie door tinkled, and Tom's gaze flicked over Lacey's shoulder. She watched his expression turn to a grimace before he returned his gaze to meet hers again.

"Great," he muttered under his breath. "I'd been wondering when my turn would come for Tweedle-dee and Tweedle-dum to pay a visit. You'll have to excuse me."

He stood, and went round from the back of the counter.

Curious to see who could elicit such a visceral response from Tom—a man who was notoriously easygoing and personable—Lacey swiveled in her stool.

The customers who'd entered the patisserie were a man and woman, and they looked like they'd just walked off the set of Dallas. The man was in a powder blue suit with a cowboy hat. The woman—much younger, Lacey noted wryly, as seemed to be the preference of most middle-aged men—was in a fuchsia pink two-piece, bright enough to give Lacey a headache, and which clashed terribly with her Dolly Parton yellow hair.

"We'd like to try some samples," the man barked. He was American, and his abruptness seemed so out of place in Tom's quaint little patisserie.

Gosh, I hope I don't sound like that to Tom, Lacey thought a little self-consciously.

"Of course," Tom replied politely, the Britishness in his own tone seeming to have intensified in response. "What would you like to try? We have pastries and..."

"Ew, Buck, no," the woman said to her husband, yanking on his arm to which she was clinging. "You know wheat makes me bloat. Ask him for something different."

Lacey couldn't help but raise an eyebrow at the odd pair. Was the wife incapable of asking her own questions?

"Got any chocolate?" the man she'd referred to as Buck asked. Or, more like demanded, since his tone was so boorish.

"I do," Tom said, somehow keeping his cool in front of Loudmouth and his limpet of a wife.

He showed them over to the chocolate display and gestured with a hand. Buck grabbed one in his meaty fist and shoved it straight into his mouth.

Almost immediately, he spit it back out. The little gooey, half-chewed lump splattered onto the floor.

Chester, who'd been very quietly sitting at Lacey's feet, suddenly sprang up and launched for it.

"Chester. No," Lacey warned him in the firm, authoritative voice he knew full well he had to obey. "Poison."

The English Shepherd looked at her, then mournfully back at the chocolate, before finally going back to his position at her feet with the expression of a scorned child.

"Ew, Buck, there's a dog in here!" the blond woman wailed. "It's so unhygienic."

"Hygiene is the least of his troubles," Buck scoffed, looking back at Tom, who was now wearing a slightly mortified expression. "Your chocolate tastes like garbage!"

"American chocolate and English chocolate are different," Lacey said, feeling the need to jump in to Tom's defense.

"You don't say," Buck replied. "It tastes like crap! And the queen eats this junk? She needs some proper American imports if you ask me."

Somehow, Tom managed to remain calm, though Lacey was seething enough for the both of them.

The brute of a man and his simpering wretch of a wife swirled out of the store and Tom fetched a tissue to wipe up the spit out chocolate mess they'd left behind.

"They were so rude," Lacey said incredulously, as Tom cleaned.

"They're staying at Carol's B'n'B," he explained, looking up at her from his hands and knees as he circled the rag over the tiles. "She said they're awful. The man, Buck, sends every single meal he orders back to the kitchen. After he's eaten half of it, mind you. The wife keeps claiming the shampoos and soaps are giving her a rash, but whenever Carol supplies her with something new, the originals have mysteriously disappeared." He stood up, shaking his head. "They're making everyone's life a misery."

"Huh," Lacey said, popping the last bit of croissant into her mouth. "I should count myself lucky, then. I doubt they have any interest in antiques."

Tom patted the counter. "Touch wood, Lacey. You don't want to jinx yourself."

Lacey was about to say she didn't believe in such a superstition, but then she thought of the elderly man and the ballerina from earlier, and decided it was better not to tempt fate. She tapped the countertop.

"There. The jinx is officially broken. Now, I'd better go. I still have tons of stuff to value before the auction tomorrow."

The bell above the door tinkled and Lacey looked over to see a large group of kids come hurtling inside. They were dressed in party frocks and were wearing hats. Amongst them, a small, tubby blonde child dressed as a princess and carrying a helium balloon, yelled to no one in particular, "It's my birthday!"

Lacey turned back to Tom with a small smirk on her lips. "Looks like you're about to have your hands full here."

He looked stunned, and more than a little apprehensive.

Lacey hopped off the stool, pecked Tom on the lips, then left him at the mercy of a bunch of eight-year-old girls.

Back in her store, Lacey got on with valuing the last of the Navy items for tomorrow's auction.

She was particularly thrilled with a sextant she'd sourced from the most unlikely of locations; a charity store. She'd only gone in to buy the retro games console they had displayed in the window—something she knew her computer-obsessed nephew Frankie would love—when she spotted it. An early nineteenth-century, mahogany-cased, ebony-handled, double-framed sextant! It was just sitting there on the shelf, amongst novelty mugs and some vomit-inducingly cute models of teddy bears.

Lacey hadn't quite believed her eyes. She was an antiques novice, after all. Such a find must've been wishful thinking. But when she'd rushed over to inspect it, the underside of its base had been inscribed with the words 'Bate, Poultry, London', which confirmed to her she was holding a genuine, rare Robert Brettell Bate!

Lacey had called Percy straight away, knowing he was the only person in the world who'd be as excited as she was. She'd been right. The man had sounded like all his Christmases had come early.

"What are you going to do with it?" he asked. "You'll have to hold an auction. A rare item like that can't just be popped on eBay. It deserves fanfare."

While Lacey had been surprised someone Percy's age knew what eBay was, her mind attached to the word *auction*. Could she do it? Hold another one so soon after the first? She'd had an entire estate's worth of Victorian furniture to sell before. She couldn't just hold an auction for this one item. Besides, it felt immoral to buy a rare antique from a charity store, knowing its true value.

"I know," Lacey said, hitting on an idea. "I'll use the sextant as a lure, as the main attraction of a general auction. Then whatever proceeds I make from its sale can go back to the charity shop."

That would solve two dilemmas; the icky feeling of buying something under its true value from a charity, and what to do with it once she had.

And so that's how the whole plan had come together. Lacey had bought the sextant (and the console, which she'd dropped in her excitement and almost forgotten to pick back up), decided on a naval theme, then got to work curating the auction and spread the buzz about it.

The sound of the bell over the door pulled Lacey from her reverie. She looked up to see her gray-haired, cardigan-clad neighbor, Gina, waltzing in with Boudicca, her Border Collie, in tow.

"What are you doing here?" Lacey asked. "I thought we were meeting for lunch."

"We are!" Gina replied, pointing at the large brass and wrought iron clock hanging on the wall.

Lacey glanced over. Along with everything in the "Nordic corner," the clock was amongst her favorite decorative features in the store. It was an antique (of course), and looked like it might have once been attached to the front of a Victorian workhouse.

"Oh!" Lacey exclaimed, finally noticing the time. "It's one-thirty. Already? The day's flown by."

It was the first time the two friends had planned to close up shop for an hour and have a proper lunch together. And by "planned," what really had happened was Gina had plied Lacey with too much wine one evening and twisted her arm until she caved and agreed to it. It was true that pretty much every local and visitor in Wilfordshire town spent the lunch hour inside a cafe or pub anyway, rather than perusing the shelves of an antiques store, and that the hour closure was very unlikely to dent Lacey's trade, but now that Lacey had learned it was a bank holiday Monday, she started second-guessing herself.

"Maybe it's not a good idea after all," Lacey said.

Gina put her hands on her hips. "Why? What excuse have you come up with this time?"

"Well, I didn't realize it was a bank holiday today. There are tons more people around than usual."

"Tons more people, not tons more *customers*," Gina said. "Because every single one of them will be sitting inside a cafe or pub or coffee shop in about ten minutes' time, just like we should be! Come on, Lacey. We talked about this. No one buys antiques over lunchtime!"

"But what if some of them are Europeans?" Lacey said. "You know they do everything later on the continent. If they have dinner at nine or ten p.m., then what time do they have lunch? Probably not one!"

Gina took her by the shoulders. "You're right. But they spend the lunch hour having a siesta instead. If there are any European tourists, they'll be asleep for the next hour. To put it into words you might understand, *not shopping in an antiques store!*"

"Okay, fine. So the Europeans will be sleeping. But what if they've come from further afield and their biological clocks are still out of sync, so they're not hungry for lunch and feel like shopping for antiques instead?"

Gina just folded her arms. "Lacey," she said, in a motherly way. "You need a break. You'll run yourself into the ground if you spend every minute of every day inside these four walls, however artfully decorated they may be."

Lacey twisted her lips. Then she placed the sextant down on the counter and headed for the shop floor. "You're right. How much harm can one hour really do?"

They were words Lacey would soon come to regret.

CHAPTER THREE

"I've been dying to visit the new tearoom," Gina said exuberantly, as she and Lacey strolled along the seafront, their canine companions racing one another through the surf, wagging their tails with excitement.

"Why?" Lacey asked. "What's so good about it?"

"Nothing in particular," Gina replied. She lowered her voice. "It's just that I heard the new owner used to be a pro-wrestler! I can't wait to meet him."

Lacey couldn't help herself. She tipped her head back and guffawed at just how ludicrous a rumor it was. But, then again, it hadn't been that long ago that everyone in Wilfordshire thought she might be a murderer.

"How about we take that hearsay with a pinch of salt?" she suggested to Gina.

Her friend "pfft" her, and the two set about giggling.

The beach was looking particularly attractive in the warmer weather. It wasn't quite hot enough for sunbathing or paddling, but plenty more people were starting to walk along it, and buy ice creams from the trucks. As they went, the two friends fell into easy chatter, and Lacey filled Gina in with the whole David phone call, and the touching story of the man and the ballerina. Then they reached the tearoom.

It was housed in what was once a canoe garage, in a prime seafront location. The prior owners had been the ones to convert it, turning the old shed into a somewhat dingy cafe—something Gina had taught her was referred to in England as a "greasy spoon." But the new owner had vastly improved on the design. They'd cleaned the brick frontage, removing streaks of seagull poop that had probably been there since the fifties. They'd put a chalkboard outside, proclaiming *organic coffee* in the cursive writing of a professional sign writer. And the original wooden doors had been replaced by a shiny glass one.

Gina and Lacey approached. The door swished open automatically, as if to beckon them inside. They exchanged a glance and went in.

The pungent smell of fresh coffee beans greeted them, followed by the scent of wood, wet soil, and metal. Gone were the old floor to ceiling white tiles, the pink vinyl booths, and linoleum flooring. Now, all the old brickwork had been exposed and the old floorboards had been varnished with a dark stain. Keeping up with the rustic vibe, all the tables and chairs appeared to be made from the planks of reclaimed fishing boats—which accounted for the smell of wood—and copper piping concealed all the wiring of several large, Edison-style bulbs that hung down from the high ceiling—accounting for the metallic smell. The earthy smell was caused by the fact that every spare inch of space had a cactus in it.

Gina gripped Lacey's arm and whispered with displeasure, "Oh no. It's ... *trendy!*"

Lacey had recently learned during an antique-buying trip to Shoreditch in London that *trendy* was not a compliment to be used in the place of 'stylish', but rather had a subtext off frivolous, pretentious and arrogant.

"I like it," Lacey countered. "It's very well designed. Even Saskia would agree."

"Careful. You don't want to get pricked," Gina added, making an exaggerated swerving motion to avoid a large prickly-looking cactus.

Lacey "tsked" her and went up to the counter, which was made of burnished bronze, and had a matching old coffee machine that surely must be decorative. Despite what Gina had heard, there wasn't a man who resembled a wrestler standing behind it, but a woman with a choppy, dyed blond bob and a white tank top that complemented her golden skin and bulging biceps.

Gina caught Lacey's eye and nodded at the woman's muscles in a *see, I told you so,* way.

"What can I get ya?" the woman asked in the thickest Aussie accent Lacey had ever heard.

Before Lacey had a chance to ask for a cortado, Gina nudged her in the ribs.

"She's like you!" Gina exclaimed. "An American!"

Lacey couldn't stop herself from laughing. "Erm ... no, she's not."

"I'm from Australia," the woman corrected Gina, good-naturedly.

"Are you?" Gina asked, looking perplexed. "But you sound exactly like Lacey to me."

The blond woman instantly flicked her gaze back to Lacey.

"Lacey?" she repeated, as if she'd already heard of her. "*You're* Lacey?"

"Uh ... yeah ...." Lacey said, feeling quite odd that this stranger somehow knew about her.

"You own the antiques store, right?" the woman added, putting down the little notepad she'd been holding and shoving her pencil behind her ear. She stuck out her hand.

Feeling even more bemused, Lacey nodded and took the hand being offered to her. The woman had a strong grip. Lacey briefly wondered whether there was any truth to the wrestling rumors after all.

"Sorry, but how do you know who I am?" Lacey queried, as the woman pumped her arm up and down vigorously with a wide grin on her face.

"Because every local person who comes in here and realizes I'm a foreigner immediately goes on to tell me all about you! About how you also moved here from abroad on your own. And how you started your own store from scratch. I think the whole of Wilfordshire is rooting for us to become best friends."

She was still shaking Lacey's hand vigorously, and when Lacey spoke, her voice shook from the vibration.

"So you came to the UK alone then?"

Finally, the woman let go of her hand.

"Yeah. I divorced my hubby, then realized divorcing him wasn't enough. Really, I needed to be on the other side of the planet to him."

Lacey couldn't help but laugh. "Same. Well, similar. New York isn't exactly the other side of the planet, but with the way Wilfordshire is, sometimes it feels like it may as well be."

Gina cleared her throat. "Can I get a cappuccino and a tuna melt?"

The woman seemed to suddenly remember Gina was there. "Oh. I'm sorry. Where are my manners?" She offered her hand to Gina. "I'm Brooke."

Gina didn't make eye contact. She shook Brooke's hand limply. Lacey picked up on the vibes of jealousy she was giving off and couldn't help but smile to herself.

"Gina's my partner in crime," Lacey told Brooke. "She works with me in my store, helps me find stock, takes my dog for playdates, imparts all her gardening wisdom to me, and generally has kept me sane ever since I came to Wilfordshire."

Gina's jealous pout was replaced by a sheepish smile.

Brooke smiled. "I hope I get my own Gina, too," she joked. "It's a pleasure to meet you both."

She retrieved the pencil from behind her ear, making her sleek blond hair swish back into place. "So that's one cappuccino and tuna melt..." she said, writing on the notebook. "And for you?" She looked up at Lacey with expectancy in her gaze.

"A cortado," Lacey said, looking down at the menu. She quickly scanned everything on offer. There was a wide array of very tasty-sounding dishes, but really the menu consisted solely of sandwiches with fancy descriptions. The tuna melt Gina had ordered was in fact a 'skipjack tuna and oak-smoked cheddar toastie'. "Erm... The smashed avo baguette."

Brooke noted the order down.

"What about your furry friends?" she added, pointing her pencil between Gina and Lacey's shoulders to where Boudicca and Chester were pacing around in a figure eight motion in their attempts to sniff one another. "Bowl of water and some doggie kibble?"

"That would be great," Lacey said, impressed by how accommodating the woman was.

She would make a great hotelier, Lacey thought. Maybe her job back in Australia had been in hospitality? Or maybe she was just a nice person. Either way, she'd made a great first impression on Lacey. Perhaps the Wilfordshire locals would get their way and the two would go on to become firm friends. Lacey could always do with more allies!

She and Gina headed off to choose a table. Amongst the vintage patio furniture, they had the option of sitting at a table made of a door on its side, thrones made out of tree stumps, or one of the nooks, which were made from the halves of sawn up rowing boats filled with pillows. They went for the safe option—a wooden picnic table.

"She seems absolutely lovely," Lacey said, as she slid to seating.

Gina shrugged and flopped down on the bench opposite. "Meh. She seemed *alright*."

She'd gone back to jealously pouting.

"You know you're my fave," Lacey told Gina.

"For now. What about when you and Brooke buddy up to chat about being expats?"

"I can have more than one friend."

"I know that. It's just, who will you end up wanting to spend more time with? Someone your own age who owns a trendy store, or someone old enough to be your mother who smells of sheep?"

Lacey couldn't help but laugh, though it was without malice. She reached across the table and squeezed Gina's hand.

"I meant it when I said you keep me sane. Honestly, with everything that happened with Iris, and the police and Taryn's attempts to drive me out of Wilfordshire, I really would've lost my mind if it hadn't been for you. You're a good friend, Gina, and I don't take that for granted. I'm not going to abandon you just because a cactus-wielding ex-wrestler's arrived in town. Okay?"

"A cactus-wielding ex-wrestler?" said Brooke, appearing beside them holding a tray of coffees and sandwiches. "You wouldn't be talking about me, would you?"

Lacey's cheeks went instantly hot. It wasn't like her to gossip about people behind their backs. She'd only been trying to cheer Gina up.

"Ha! Lacey, your face!" Brooke exclaimed, thumping her on the back. "It's fine. I don't mind. I'm proud of my past."

"You mean to say..."

"Yup," Brooke said, grinning. "It's true. There's really not as much of a story there, though, as people have made out. I wrestled in high school, then college, before doing a year-long stint professionally. I guess small-town English folk think it's more exotic than it is."

Lacey felt very silly now. Of course everything could be blown out of proportion and distorted as it was passed from one person to the next along the small town gossip system. Brooke being a wrestler in the past was as much of a non-event as Lacey having worked as an interior designer's assistant in New York; normal for her, exotic for everyone else.

"Now, as for wielding cactuses..." Brooke said. Then she gave Lacey a wink.

She decanted the food from the tray to the table, fetched bowls of water and kibble for the dogs, then left Lacey and Gina to eat in peace.

Despite the overly complicated description on the menu, the food was actually terrific. The avocado was perfectly ripened, softened enough to lose its bite but not too soft as to be mushy. The bread was fresh, seeded, and nicely toasted. In fact, it even rivaled Tom's and that was the highest praise Lacey could really give anything! The coffee was the real triumph though. Lacey had been drinking tea these days, since it was constantly being offered to her, and because there wasn't a local place that seemed to match up to her standards. But Brooke's coffee tasted like it had been shipped straight here from Colombia! Lacey would *definitely* switch to getting her morning coffee from here, on the days when she started work at a sensible hour rather than at a time when most sane people were still snoozing in bed.

Lacey was halfway through her lunch when the automatic door behind her swished open and in waltzed none other than Buck and his silly wife. Lacey groaned.

"Hey, chick," Buck said, clicking his fingers at Brooke and thudding down into a seat. "We need coffee. And I'll take a steak and fries." He pointed at the tabletop in a demanding way, then looked over at his wife. "Daisy? What do you want?"

The woman was hovering at the door on her tippy-toed stilettos, looking somewhat terrified of all the cactuses.

"I'll just have whatever has the least carbs in," she murmured.

"A salad for the missus," Buck barked at Brooke. "Easy on the dressing."

Brooke flashed Lacey and Gina a look, then went off to make her rude customers' orders.

Lacey buried her face in her hands, feeling secondhand embarrassment for the couple. She really hoped the people of Wilfordshire didn't think all Americans were like this. Buck and Daisy were giving her entire country a bad name.

"Great," Lacey muttered as Buck began loudly talking at his wife. "These two ruined my tea date with Tom. Now they're ruining my lunch break with you."

Gina looked unimpressed with the pair. "I've got an idea," she said.

She bent down and whispered something to Boudicca that made her ears twitch. Then she released the dog from her leash. She went pelting across the tearooms, leapt at the table, and grabbed the steak clean off Buck's plate.

"HEY!" he bellowed.

Brooke couldn't help herself. She burst out laughing.

Lacey gasped, amused by Gina's antics.

"Get me another," Buck demanded. "And get that dog OUT."

"I'm sorry, but that was my last steak," Brooke said, flashing a subtle wink at Lacey.

The couple huffed and stormed out.

The three women burst out laughing.

"That wasn't your last at all, was it?" Lacey asked.

"Nah," Brooke said, chuckling. "I've got a whole freezer stuffed full of them!"

⚜ ⚜ ⚜

It was drawing up toward the end of the workday and Lacey had finished valuing all of the naval items for tomorrow's auction. She was so excited.

That was, until the bell rang and in waltzed Buck and Daisy.

Lacey groaned. She wasn't as calm as Tom, and she wasn't as jovial at Brooke. She really didn't think this meeting would go well.

"Look at all this junk," Buck said to his wife. "What a load of nothin'. Why did you even want to come in here, Daisy? And it smells." His eyes went over to Chester. "It's that disgusting dog again!"

Lacey clenched her teeth so hard she half expected them to crack. She tried to channel Tom's calm as she approached the pair.

"I'm afraid Wilfordshire is a very small town," she said. "You'll run into the same people—and dogs—all the time."

"It's you," Daisy asked, evidently recognizing Lacey from their two earlier run-ins. "This is your store?" She had a ditzy voice, like your average Valley Girl airhead.

"It is," Lacey confirmed, feeling increasingly wary. Daisy's question had felt loaded, like an accusation.

"When I heard your accent in the patisserie, I figured you were a customer," Daisy continued. "But you actually *live* here?" She pulled a face. "What made you want to leave America for *this*?"

Lacey felt every single muscle in her body tense. Her blood started to boil.

"Probably for the same reasons you chose to vacation here," Lacey replied in the calmest voice she could muster. "The beach. The ocean. The countryside. The charming architecture."

"Daisy," Buck barked. "Can you hurry up and find that thing you dragged me in here to buy?"

Daisy glanced over at the counter. "It's gone." She looked at Lacey. "Where's the brass thing that was over there before?"

Brass thing? Lacey thought back to the items she'd been working on before Gina's arrival.

Daisy continued. "It's like a sort of compass, with a telescope attached. For boats. I saw it through the window when the store was closed over lunch. Did you sell it already?"

"Do you mean the sextant?" she asked, frowning with confusion over what a ditzy blond like Daisy would want with an antique sextant.

"That's it!" Daisy exclaimed. "A sextant."

Buck guffawed. Obviously the name amused him.

"Don't you get enough sextant at home?" he quipped.

Daisy giggled, but it sounded forced to Lacey, less like she was actually amused and more like she was just being accommodating.

Lacey herself was not amused. She folded her arms and raised her eyebrows.

"I'm afraid the sextant is not for sale," she explained, keeping her focus on Daisy rather than Buck, who was making it very hard for her to stay personable. "All my naval items are going to be auctioned tomorrow, so it's not for general sale."

Daisy stuck out her bottom lip. "But I want it. Buck will pay double what it's worth. Won't you, Bucky?" She tugged on his arm.

Before Buck had a chance to respond, Lacey interjected. "No, I'm sorry, that's not possible. I don't know how much I'll fetch for it. That's the whole point of the auction. It's a rare piece, and there are specialists coming from all over the country just to bid on it. The price could be anything. If I sold it to you now, I may lose out, and since the proceeds are going to charity, I want to secure the best deal."

A deep furrow appeared across Buck's forehead. In that moment, Lacey felt even more aware of just how big and wide the man really was. He was well over six feet, and thicker than two of her put together, like a large oak tree. He was intimidating, in both size and mannerism.

"Did you not just hear what my wife said?" he barked. "She wants to buy your thingamajig so name your price."

"I heard her," Lacey replied, standing her ground. "It's me who's not being listened to. The sextant is not for sale."

She sounded far more confident than she felt. A small alarm bell in the back of her mind started ringing, telling her she was plowing headfirst into a dangerous situation.

Buck took a step forward, his looming shadow stretching over her. Chester leapt up and growled in response, but Buck clearly wasn't fazed and just ignored him.

"You're refusing me sale?" he said. "Isn't that illegal? Isn't our money good enough for you?" He pulled a pile of cash from his pocket and waved it under Lacey's nose in a decidedly threatening manner. "It's got the Queen's face on it and everything. Isn't that enough for you?"

Chester began to bark furiously. Lacey gave him a hand signal to stop, and he did, obediently, but he still held his position as if he were ready to attack the second she gave him the go ahead.

Lacey folded her arms and squared off to Buck, aware of every inch he loomed over her but determined to hold her ground. She wasn't going to be bullied into selling the sextant. She wasn't going to let this mean, hulking man intimidate her and ruin the auction she'd worked so hard for and was so looking forward to.

"If you want to buy the sextant, then you'll have to come to the auction and bid on it," she said.

"Oh, I will," Buck said through narrowed eyes. He pointed right in Lacey's face. "You bet I will. Mark my words. Buckland Stringer *will* win."

With that, the couple left, swirling out the store so fast they practically left turbulence in their wake. Chester ran to the window, put his front paws up against the glass, and growled at their retreating backs. Lacey watched them go, too, until they were out of sight. It was only then she noticed how much her heart was racing, and how much her legs were trembling. She gripped the countertop to steady herself.

Tom had been right. She'd jinxed herself by saying the pair had no reason to come to her store. But she could be forgiven for assuming there was nothing of interest for them in here. No one would have been able to guess by looking at her that Daisy had any desire to own an antique navy sextant!

"Oh, Chester," Lacey said, sinking her head into her fist. "Why did I tell them about the auction?"

The dog whined, picking up on the note of mournful regret in her tone.

"Now I have to put up with them tomorrow as well!" she exclaimed. "And what's the likelihood they know anything of auction etiquette? It's going to be a disaster."

And just like that, her excitement for her auction tomorrow was dowsed like a flame between fingertips. In its place, Lacey felt only dread.

CHAPTER FOUR

After her encounter with Buck and Daisy, Lacey was more than ready to lock up for the day and head home. Tom was coming over tonight to cook for her, and she was really looking forward to curling up on the couch with a glass of wine and a movie. But there was still the till to balance, and stock to tidy, the floors to sweep and the coffee machine to clean . . . Not that Lacey was complaining. She loved her store and everything that went along with owning it.

When she was finally finished, she headed for the exit, Chester in tow, noticing that the hands on the wrought iron clock had reached 7 p.m., and outside it was dark. Though spring had brought longer days with it, Lacey had yet to enjoy any of them. But she could feel the change in the atmosphere; the town seemed more vibrant, with many of the cafes and pubs staying open longer, and people sitting on the tables outside drinking coffee and beer. It gave the place a festive vibe.

Lacey locked up her store. She'd become extra diligent since the break-in, but even if that had never happened, she'd have gotten this way, because the store felt like her child now. It was something that needed to be nurtured and protected and cared for. In such a short space of time, she'd fallen completely in love with the place

"Who knew you could fall in love with a store?" she mused aloud with a deep sigh of satisfaction for the way her life had turned out.

From beside her, Chester whinnied.

Lacey patted his head. "Yes, I'm in love with you too, don't worry!"

At the mention of love, she remembered the plans she had with Tom that evening, and gazed over at his patisserie.

To her surprise, she saw all the lights were on. It was most unusual. Tom had to open his store at the inhuman hour of 5 a.m. to make sure everything was ready for the breakfast crowd at 7, which meant he usually closed at 5 p.m. on the dot. But it was 7 p.m. and he was clearly still inside. The sandwich board was still out in the street. The sign in the door was still turned to open.

"Come on, Chester," Lacey said to her furry companion. "Let's see what's going on."

They crossed the street together and went inside the patisserie.

Right away, Lacey could hear something of a commotion coming from the kitchen. It sounded like the usual sounds of clattering pots and pans, but in hyperdrive.

"Tom?" she called out, a little nervously.

"Hey!" his disembodied voice came from the back kitchen. He used his normal sunny tone.

Now that Lacey knew he wasn't in the middle of being burglarized by a macaron thief, she relaxed. She hopped onto her usual stool, as the clattering continued.

"Everything okay back there?" she asked.

"Fine!" Tom called in response.

A moment later, he finally appeared in the archway of the kitchenette. He had his apron on, and it—as well as most of his clothes underneath and his hair—were covered in flour. "There's been a minor disaster."

"Minor?" Lacey mocked. Now that she knew Tom wasn't fighting off a kitchen intruder, she could appreciate the humor in the situation.

"It was Paul, actually," Tom began.

"What's he done *now*?" Lacey asked, recalling the time Tom's trainee had accidentally used baking soda instead of flour in a batch of dough rendering the entirety of it unusable.

Tom held up two almost identical-looking white packages. On the left, the faded printed label read: sugar. On the right: salt.

"Ah," Lacey said.

Tom nodded. "Yup. It's the batch for tomorrow morning's breakfast pastries. I'm going to have to remake the whole lot, or risk the angry wrath of the locals when they arrive for breakfast and discover I have nothing to sell them."

"Does that mean you're cancelling our plans tonight?" Lacey asked. The humor she'd felt moments earlier was suddenly dashed, and now in its place she felt heavy disappointment.

Tom flashed her an apologetic look. "I'm so sorry. Let's reschedule. Tomorrow? I'll come over and cook for you."

"I can't," Lacey replied. "I'm having that meeting with Ivan tomorrow."

"The Crag Cottage sale meeting," Tom said, snapping his fingers. "Of course. I remember. How about Wednesday evening?"

"Aren't you heading off for that focaccia course Wednesday?"

Tom looked perturbed. He checked the calendar hanging up, then let out a sigh. "Okay, that's *next* Wednesday." He chuckled. "You gave me a fright. Oh, but I am busy Wednesday evening after all. And Thursday—"

"—is badminton practice," Lacey finished for him.

"Which means I'm next free on Friday. Is Friday good?"

His tone was just as happy-go-lucky as usual, Lacey noted, but his blasé attitude over cancelling their plans together stung her. He didn't seem to mind at all that they may not be able to see one another in a romantic capacity until the end of the week.

Though Lacey knew full well she had no plans on Friday, she still heard herself saying, "I'll have to check my diary and get back to you."

And no sooner had the words left her lips than a new emotion crept into her stomach, mixing with the disappointment. To Lacey's surprise, the emotion was relief.

Relief that she wouldn't be able to have a romantic date with Tom for a week? She couldn't quite comprehend where the relief was coming from, and it made her feel suddenly guilty.

"Sure," Tom said, seemingly oblivious. "We can put a pin in it for now and arrange to do something extra special next time, when we're both less busy?" He paused for her response, and when it didn't come, added, "Lacey?"

She snapped back to the moment. "Yes . . . Right. Sounds good."

Tom came over and leaned his elbows onto the counter, so their faces were level. "Now. Serious question. Are you going to be alright for food tonight? Because obviously you were expecting a tasty, nutritious meal. I have some meat pies that didn't sell today, if you want to take one home with you?"

Lacey chuckled and smacked his arm. "I don't need your handouts, thank you very much! I'll have you know I can actually cook!"

"Oh really?" Tom teased.

"I've been known to make a dish or two in my time," Lacey told him. "Mushroom risotto. Seafood paella." She racked her brains for at least one other thing to add, because everyone knew you needed at least three for a list! "Um...um..."

Tom raised his eyebrows. "Go on...?"

"Macaroni and cheese!" Lacey exclaimed.

Tom laughed heartily. "That's quite an impressive repertoire. And yet I've never seen any evidence to support your claims."

He was right about that. So far, Tom had made all the meals for them. It made sense. He loved cooking, and he had the skills to pull it off. Lacey's culinary skills weren't much above piercing the film of a microwavable dish.

She folded her arms. "I haven't exactly had the chance to yet," she replied, using the same jokingly argumentative tone as Tom in the hopes it would mask the genuine irritation his comment had roused in her. "Mr. Michelin Star pastry chef doesn't trust me near the stove."

"Should I take that as an offer?" Tom asked, wiggling his eyebrows.

Damn pride, Lacey thought. She'd walked right into that one. *Way to set yourself up.*

"You bet," she said, feigning confidence. She held her hand out to him to shake. "Challenge accepted."

Tom looked at her hand without moving, twisting his lips to the side. "There's one condition, though."

"Oh? What's that?"

"It has to be something traditional. Something native to New York."

"In that case, you've just made my job ten times easier," Lacey exclaimed. "Because that means I'll be making pizza and cheesecake."

"Nothing can be store bought," Tom added. "The whole thing has to be made from scratch. And no getting any sneaky help. No asking Paul for the pastry."

"Oh please," Lacey said, pointing at the discarded salt bag on the counter. "Paul is the last person I'd enlist to help me cheat."

Tom laughed. Lacey nudged her extended hand closer to him. He nodded to indicate he was satisfied that she'd meet the conditions, then took her hand. But instead of shaking it he gave it a small tug, bringing her closer toward him, and kissed her over the counter.

"I'll see you tomorrow," Lacey murmured, the tingle from his lips echoing on hers. "Through the window, I mean. Unless you have time to come to the auction?"

"Of course I'm coming to the auction," Tom told her. "I missed the last one. I need to be there to support you."

She smiled. "Great."

She turned and headed for the exit, leaving Tom to his mess of pastry.

As soon as the patisserie's door shut behind her, she looked down at Chester.

"I've really landed myself in it now," she said to her perceptive-looking dog. "Really, you should've stopped me. Tugged on my sleeve. Nudged me with your nose. Anything. But now I've got to make pizza from scratch. And a cheesecake! Shoot." She scuffed her shoe on the sidewalk with faux frustration. "Come on, we'll have to go grocery shopping before we go home."

Lacey turned the opposite direction to home, and hurried down the high street toward the grocery store (or *corner shop* as Gina insisted on calling it). As she went, she put a message on the *Doyle Girlz* thread.

Anyone know how to make cheesecake?

Surely it was the sort of thing her mom would just know how to do, right?

It wasn't long before she heard her cell ping in reply, and she checked to see who had responded. Unfortunately, it was her infamously sarcastic little sister, Naomi.

You don't, her sister quipped. *You buy it premade and save the hassle.*

Lacey quickly tapped out a reply. *Not helpful, sis.*

Naomi's response came in lightning-quick speed. *If you ask stupid questions, expect stupid answers.*

Lacey rolled her eyes and hurried on.

Luckily, by the time Lacey reached the store, her mom messaged back with a recipe.

It's Martha Stewart's, she wrote. *You can trust her.*

Trust her? Naomi tapped in response. *Didn't she go to jail?*

Yes, their Mom replied. *But that had nothing to do with her cheesecake recipe.*

Touché, Naomi replied.

Lacey laughed. Mom had actually outdone Naomi!

She put her phone away, tied Chester's leash around the lamppost, then headed inside the brightly lit store. She whizzed about as quickly as she could, filing her basket with everything Martha Stewart told her she needed, then grabbed herself a precooked bag of linguine pasta and a small tub of premade sauce (which was conveniently placed in the fridge right beside it), and some pre-shaven parmesan cheese (located beside the sauce), before finally grabbing the bottle of wine beneath that proclaimed; *goes great with linguine!*

No wonder I never really learned to cook, Lacey thought. *Look how easy they make it.*

She went to the till, paid for her goods, then left, collecting Chester on the way out. They went back past her store—she noticed Tom was right where she'd left him—and collected the car from the side street where Lacey had parked.

It was a short drive to Crag Cottage, along the seafront then up the cliffside. Chester sat alert in the passenger seat beside her, and as the car crested over the hill, Crag Cottage came into view. A feeling of delight swelled inside Lacey. The cottage really felt like home. And after tomorrow's meeting with Ivan, she'd possibly be one step closer to becoming its official owner.

Just then, she noticed the warm glow of a bonfire coming from the direction of Gina's cottage, and decided to head past her house and along the bumpy, single-track path to her neighbor.

As she pulled to a halt, she could see the woman standing in her wellies beside the fire, which she was adding foliage to. The fire looked very pretty in the dusky spring evening light.

Lacey tooted the car horn and wound down the stiff window.

Gina turned and waved. "Hey-ho Lacey. Do you need to burn something?"

Lacey leaned out the window on her elbows. "Nope. Just wondering if you wanted some help?"

"I thought you had a date with Tom tonight?" Gina asked.

"I did," Lacey told her, feeling that odd mixture of disappointment and relief stirring in her gut again. "But he cancelled. Pastry-related emergency."

"Ah," Gina said. She dumped another tree branch onto the bonfire, making sparks of red, orange and yellow fly into the air. "Well, I've got everything here covered, thanks. Unless you've got some marshmallows you want to toast?"

"Darn, no, I don't. That sounds nice! And I just went grocery shopping!"

She decided to blame her lack of marshmallows on Martha Stewart and her extremely sensible vanilla cheesecake recipe.

Lacey was about to wish Gina a good night and reverse her car back the way she'd come, when she felt Chester nudging her with his nose. She turned and looked over at him. The shopping bags that she'd placed in the passenger footwell had spilled open, and some of the items she'd brought had fallen out.

"That's an idea..." Lacey said. She looked back out the window. "Hey, Gina. How about we have dinner together? I have wine and pasta. And all the ingredients to make Martha Stewart's authentic New York City style cheesecake if we get bored and need an activity."

Gina looked thrilled. "You had me at wine!" she exclaimed.

Lacey laughed. She reached down to fetch the grocery bags from the footwell, and earned herself another nudge from Chester's wet nose.

"What is it now?" she asked him.

He tipped his head to the side, his fluffy tufts of eyebrow flitting upward.

"Oh. I get it," Lacey said. "I told you off before for not stopping me from putting my foot in it earlier with Tom. You're proving a point, aren't you, that it all worked out nonetheless? Well, I'll give you that."

He whinnied.

She chuckled and petted his head. "Clever boy."

She got out the car, Chester leaping out after her, and headed up Gina's path, maneuvering around the sheep and chickens that were dotted about the place.

They headed inside.

"So what happened with Tom?" Gina asked as they walked the length of the low-ceilinged corridor toward her rustic country-cottage kitchen.

"It was Paul actually," Lacey explained. "He mixed up the flours or something."

They entered the brightly lit kitchen, and Lacey placed the shopping bags on the work surface.

"It's about time he fired that Paul lad," Gina said with a *tsk*.

"He's an apprentice," Lacey told her. "He's supposed to make mistakes!"

"Sure. But then he's meant to *learn* from them. How many batches of pastry has he ruined now? And for it to impact on *your* plans really does take the biscuit."

Lacey smirked at Gina's amusing phrase.

"Honestly, it's fine," she said, taking all the items out of the bag. "I'm an independent woman. I don't need to see Tom every day."

Gina grabbed some wine glasses and poured them each a glass, then they got on with making the dinner.

"You'll never believe who came into my store before closing time today," Lacey said, as she gave the pasta a cursory stir in its pot of simmering water. The instructions said no stirring was required during the four minutes it took to boil, but that just felt too lazy, even for Lacey!

"Not the Americans?" Gina asked, in a tone of distaste as she popped the tomato sauce in the microwave for the whole two minutes it required to heat.

"Yes. The Americans."

Gina shuddered. "Oh dear. What did they want? Let me guess, Daisy wanted Buck to buy her an overpriced piece of jewelry?"

Lacey strained the pasta in a sieve, then shared it out between two bowls. "That's the thing. Daisy *did* want Buck to buy her something. The sextant."

"The sextant?" Gina asked, as she dumped the tomato sauce on top of the pasta, inelegantly. "As in the naval instrument? What would a woman like Daisy want a sextant for?"

"Right? That's exactly what I thought!" Lacey sprinkled parmesan shavings on top of her pasta mound.

"Maybe she just picked it at random," Gina mused, handing Lacey one of the two forks she'd retrieved from the cutlery drawer.

"She was very specific about it," Lacey continued. She carried her food and wine toward the table. "She wanted to buy it and of course I told her she'd have to come to the auction. I thought she'd drop it, but nope. She said she'd be there. So now I have to put up with the two of them again tomorrow. If only I'd put the damn thing away rather than leaving it out in plain view of the window over lunch!"

She looked up as Gina took her seat opposite, to see that her neighbor was looking quite flustered all of a sudden. She didn't seem to have anything to add to what Lacey had said, either, which was extremely uncharacteristic for the usually chatty woman.

"What is it?" Lacey asked. "What's wrong?"

"Well, I was the one who convinced you that closing up shop for lunch wouldn't hurt," Gina mumbled. "But it did. Because it gave Daisy the chance to see the sextant! It's my fault."

Lacey laughed. "Don't be silly. Come on, let's eat before this goes cold and all our effort goes to waste."

"Wait. We need one more thing." Gina went over to her herb pots lined up on the window ledge and picked some leaves off one. "Fresh basil!" She placed a sprig on each of their bowls of badly presented, gloopy pasta. "Et voila!"

For all its cheap cheerfulness, it was actually a very tasty meal. But then again, most convenience foods are filled with fat and sugar, so it would have to be!

"Am I a decent enough substitute for Tom?" Gina asked as they ate and drank wine.

"Tom who?" Lacey joked. "Oh, you just reminded me! Tom sort of challenged me to cook him a meal from scratch. Something native to New York. So I'm doing a cheesecake for dessert. My mom sent me a Marth Stewart recipe. Want to help me make it?"

"Martha Stewart," Gina said, shaking her head. "I have a much better recipe."

She went over to the cupboard and began rummaging around. Then she pulled out a battered cookbook.

"This was my mother's pride and joy," she said, putting it on the table in front of Lacey. "She collected recipes for years. I have clippings in here going all the way back to the war."

"Amazing," Lacey exclaimed. "But how come you never learned to cook, if you had an expert at home?"

"*Because,*" Gina said, "I was far too busy helping my dad grow veggies in the garden. I was a proper tomboy. A daddy's girl. One of those girls that liked to get my hands dirty."

"Well, baking can certainly do that," Lacey said. "You should've seen Tom earlier. He was covered head to toe in flour."

Gina laughed. "I meant I liked to get muddy! To play with bugs. Climb trees. Fish. Cooking always seemed too feminine for my tastes."

"Better not tell Tom that," Lacey chuckled. She looked down at the recipe book. "So do you want to help me make the cheesecake, or aren't there enough worms to keep you interested?"

"I'll help," Gina said. "We can use fresh eggs. Daphne and Delilah both laid this morning."

They cleaned up their dinner and got to work on the cheesecake, following Gina's Mom's recipe rather than Martha's.

"So, other than the Americans, are you excited about the auction tomorrow?" Gina asked as she crushed up biscuits in a bowl with a potato masher.

"Excited. Nervous." Lacey swilled the wine in her glass. "Mostly nervous. Knowing me, I won't sleep a wink tonight worrying about it all."

"I have an idea," Gina said then. "Once we're done here, we should go and walk the dogs on the seafront. We can take the east route. You've not gone that way yet, have you? The sea air will tire you out and you'll sleep like a baby, mark my words."

"That's a good idea," Lacey agreed. If she went home now, she'd only fret.

As Lacey put the messy cheesecake in the fridge to chill, Gina hurried into the utility room to fetch them both rain macs. It was still quite chilly in the evenings, especially by the sea where it was more blustery.

The huge waterproof, fisherman's coat swamped Lacey. But she was glad for it when they stepped outside. It was a cool, clear, evening.

They headed down the cliff steps. The beach was deserted and quite dark. It was kind of exhilarating being down here when it was so empty, Lacey thought. It felt like they were the only people in the world.

They headed toward the sea, then turned to follow the easterly direction that Lacey hadn't had a chance yet to explore. It was fun to explore somewhere new. Being in a small town like Wilfordshire sometimes felt a little stifling.

"Hey, what's that?" Lacey asked, peering across the water at what appeared to be the silhouette of a building on an island.

"Medieval ruins," Gina said. "At low tide there's a sandbar you can walk along to reach them. Definitely worth a poke around if you can be bothered to get up that early."

"What time is low tide?" Lacey asked.

"Five a.m."

"Ouch. That's probably a bit too early for me."

"You can also get there by boat, of course," Gina explained. "If you know someone who actually owns one. But if you get stuck over there, you have to call out the volunteer lifeboat and those lads don't appreciate using their resources on clueless folk, mark my words! I've done it before and got quite a stern talking to. Luckily my gift of the gab had them all chuckling by the time we reached shore, and we're all on good terms now."

Chester began to strain on his leash, as if trying to get to the island.

"I think he knows it," Lacey said.

"Maybe his old owners used to walk him over there?" Gina suggested.

Chester barked as if in confirmation.

Lacey bent down and ruffled his fur. It had been a while since she'd really thought about Chester's old owners, and how unsettling it must have been for him to lose them so suddenly.

"How about I take you there one day?" she asked him. "I'll wake up early, just for you."

With an excited wag of the tail, Chester tipped his head back and barked at the sky.

Just as she'd predicted, Lacey struggled to sleep that night. So much for the sea air tiring her out. There was just too much swirling around her mind for her to switch off; from the Crag Cottage sale meeting with Ivan, to the auction, there was just too much to think about. And while she was excited about the auction tomorrow, she was also nervous. Not just because it was only her second time doing it, but because of the unwelcome attendees she'd have to deal with in the form of Buck and Daisy Stringer.

Maybe they won't come, she thought as she stared at the shadows on her ceiling. *Daisy will probably have found something else to demand Buck buy for her.*

But no, the woman had seemed intent on buying the sextant specifically. It obviously held some kind of personal significance for her. They would be there, Lacey was certain of it, even if just to prove a point.

Lacey listened to the sound of Chester's breathing and the waves crashing against the cliffs, letting the gentle rhythms lull her into relaxation. She'd just started dropping off when her cell phone suddenly started vibrating loudly on the wooden dresser beside her head. Its eerie green light filled the room with flashes. She was usually careful to put it on night mode but it had obviously slipped her mind tonight with everything else she was thinking about.

With a fatigued groan, Lacey flailed out with her arm and grasped the cell. She brought it close to her face, squinting to see who had decided to disturb her at this ungodly hour. The name *Mom* flashed insistently on the screen at her.

Of course, Lacey thought, sighing. Her mother must have forgotten the rule about not calling her after 6 p.m. New York time.

With a sigh, Lacey answered the call. "Mom? Is everything okay?"

From the other end of the line, there was a moment's silence. "Why do you always answer my calls like that? Why does there have to be something wrong for me to call my daughter?"

Lacey rolled her eyes and sank back against the pillow. "Because it's two in the morning in the U.K. right now, and you only ever call me when you're in a panic about something. So? What is it?"

The following silence was enough of a confirmation to Lacey that she'd hit the nail on the head.

"Mom?" she prompted.

"I was just at David's—" her mom began.

"What?" Lacey exclaimed. "*Why?*"

"To meet Eda."

Lacey's chest tightened. She'd been joking when she suggested David, Eda and her mom could bond over a mani-pedi. But by the sounds of things, the three of them actually were spending time together! Why any mother would want to maintain a relationship with her daughter's ex-husband was beyond Lacey. It was absurd!

"And?" Lacey said between her teeth. "How was she?"

"She seemed nice," her mom said. "But that's not what I was calling about. David mentioned the alimony..."

Lacey couldn't help herself. She scoffed. "Did David put you up to this? Did he ask you to call me about the money?" She didn't need to hear her mom's response because it was obvious, and so she answered her own question. "Of course he did. Because the only thing David cares about is money. Oh, and finding someone willing to incubate his children."

"Lacey," her mom said disapprovingly.

But Lacey was quite awake now, and quite alert. "Well, it's true, isn't it? Why else would he get engaged to a twenty-year-old multimillionaire heiress?"

"Is that why you didn't pay him, dear?" her mom's voice came from the other end of the line. "To get back at him for the engagement?"

"I didn't do it on purpose!" Lacey exclaimed. She was getting quite animated now. Her mom was very good at getting under her skin, and suggesting she'd deliberately chosen not to pay David his alimony had infuriated her. "There was a delay on the bank's end. I didn't realize it was a bank holiday and that the payments wouldn't go through. That's all."

"You do know that once they're married, David won't be entitled to your money anymore, don't you? I mean really he's doing you a favor by speeding things along with Eda. It will save you a fortune. The least you could do is make the payments to him on time."

Lacey had no words. All she could do was blink with utter bemusement. But the thought of not having spousal support hanging over her head for years did relieve her, not that she'd give her Mom the satisfaction of knowing that.

"Duly noted. Now, can I please get some sleep? I have a very busy day tomorrow with my auction ..."

"Auction? You didn't tell me about an auction."

"Yes, I did."

"No you didn't. I'd remember something like that."

Lacey rubbed the frown line between her eyebrows. Her mom was giving her a headache. And though she was one hundred percent certain she'd told her mom about the auction—and indeed, probably had evidence of it on the *Doyle Girlz* thread—she knew disagreeing with her mom now would just cause the conversation to go on even longer.

"Sorry, I thought I'd mentioned it," she said, backing down for the sake of her sleep. "Good night, Mom." Lacey ended the call and slumped back onto her pillow.

She managed to drift off back to sleep for a couple more hours, but was awoken again, this time by the sound of bleating.

"Those damn sheep!" Lacey yelled, jumping out of bed. She wrapped herself up in a nightgown. "Come on, Chester. You can herd, can't you?"

They went out to the front lawn where tons of Gina's sheep had escaped and were making a ruckus. Chester chased them all the way along the single-track path that linked Lacey's house to Gina's, and in through the open gate that Gina had evidently forgotten to latch, and back into their field.

By the time they made it back to the house, Lacey was wide awake. There was nothing like the brisk, fresh ocean air in the morning—*and an impending auction!*—to wake you up.

She noticed the time. 5 a.m.

"Hey, Chester," she said to the dog. "The sandbar's out. Shall we go and look at that island?"

May as well. When else would she be awake at this time?

She dressed and they headed down to the beach together, taking the right hand turn as Gina had shown her the night before. And sure enough, there was the sandbar.

In the pale blue dawn light, it looked somewhat eerie, like a ghost road that had emerged from the water thanks to some kind of spell. Not to mention that as she began to stroll across the sand, the silhouette of the medieval ruins Gina told her about appeared in the distance. It was creepy.

Chester became quite animated, wagging his tail enthusiastically the closer they got.

"You *do* know this place, don't you?" Lacey asked him.

He dragged her around by the leash, towards the grounds of the old castle. It was spooky, but beautiful. Lacey quickly snapped a photo with her cell, and put it on the *Doyle Girlz* thread. She knew the moment her mom woke up and discovered she'd been wandering through abandoned ruins alone, she'd freak, but after all that debacle over David, Lacey didn't really care.

"Let's head back now," she said to Chester.

They'd not had a chance to explore fully, but Lacey was anxious about the tide coming in and covering the sandbar, and the volunteer lifeguards deciding she wasn't worth saving, and her missing her auction.

So she turned her back on the ancient ruins, vowing she'd explore them fully someday.

She didn't know it then, but it was a decision Lacey would soon come to regret.

CHAPTER FIVE

It was a busy morning at the store, which was good for Lacey because it meant her mind was occupied and couldn't fixate on the auction that afternoon.

At midday, the bell tinkled and Gina entered. She was going to work at the counter for an hour so Lacey had time to do any last minute perfecting in the auction room. The second Lacey saw her, she felt a surge of nervous anticipation rise from her stomach up to her chest. Her heart began to beat rapidly.

"You look like you're about to pass out, girly," Gina said. "You really that nervous?"

"I guess so," Lacey said, wiping her hands on her jeans. They were suddenly feeling quite clammy.

"Are you sick?" Gina added. She peered at her. "You look awful."

"Thanks a bunch," Lacey replied. "Well, between the bottle of wine we shared last night, my mom calling at 2 a.m. and your sheep deciding to watch the sunrise from my lawn, I'm not surprised."

Gina flushed pink with embarrassment. "My sheep?" she asked, with a wince. "Did they wake you?"

"Yes. I had to get Chester to herd them home, where we discovered that *someone* had left the gate wide open."

"It's the latch," Gina said immediately. "It doesn't always hook properly."

Lacey raised an eyebrow. "Maybe I should send Ivan over to fix it."

With a noncommittal shrug, Gina swished behind the counter.

Lacey was about to head to the back room when she noticed Tom through the window, leaving his patisserie with a silver trolley. Piled up on it were about a million different pastries.

"Oh!" Lacey exclaimed.

She watched Tom push the trolley over the cobblestones—a few croissants were lost during the bumpy journey—then come inside her store.

"Tom!" Lacey exclaimed, hurrying from behind the counter toward him." You didn't make all these for the auction, did you?"

"Surprise," he said, grinning.

"But when did you—" She gasped. "Last night? Was that whole thing about the sugar and salt a ruse?"

"I knew you'd fall for it if I blamed it on Paul," he replied, looking triumphant.

Lacey was touched by the gesture. It made her feel even more guilty about her reaction to him cancelling their plans now. He'd only done it in order to surprise her, and she'd spiraled into an existential crisis.

She threw her arms around his neck and pecked his cheek. "Thank you! But promise me you won't do this again? If I put on a spread every auction, I'll get a reputation then people will start expecting it. And I'd like to spend *some* time with you once in a while."

From her place behind the desk, Gina straightened up. "Maybe you should charge, Tom," she said cheekily. "I bet those folk from the English Antiques Society would pay." She looked at Lacey. "They are coming today, aren't they?"

"Yup," Lacey said.

Just then, the door opened with a tinkle and in came the biggest bouquet of beautiful flowers.

"Oh!" Lacey exclaimed with surprise.

Gina raised her eyebrows at Tom. "Looks like you have competition."

Just then, the face of the deliverer emerged out from behind the array of pinks and whites. She was a smiley woman with shiny chestnut-brown hair pulled into a high ponytail.

She stopped beside the trolley of croissants and looked at Gina. "Lacey Doyle?"

Gina spat her laughter. "No one's bought me flowers for decades, love. That's Lacey."

She pointed at Lacey, and Lacey gave a sheepish wave.

The delivery woman turned to face her, obscuring her face once more entirely behind the oversized bouquet.

"Where shall I put these?" she asked.

It looked to Lacey as if she was being spoken to by a large bunch of flowers.

"Just here," she said, tapping the counter and turning her face to hide her smirk.

The woman placed the vase down gently on the counter, beside the plates of croissants Tom was busily transferring from the trolley.

"Who are they from?" he asked without making eye contact.

Lacey had never seen Tom look so stiff. She decided not to tease him for the evident insecurity the flowers had caused him.

Curiously, Lacey reached for the card resting within the stems, and read it aloud. "Good luck on your first solo auction. With love from . . . Oh! Percy and Karen!"

"Ah," Gina said, reaching for a croissant. "What a lovely man."

She offered a croissant to the brunette deliverer. The woman politely shook her head.

Tom seemed to visibly relax at the announcement that the flowers were from Lacey's grandfatherly auctioneering mentor rather than some mystery admirer, and immediately stopped distracting himself with his croissant transfer operation.

Lacey signed for the delivery, beyond touched that Percy, who'd been there to support her during her first ever auction, and who had inspired her to hold her second, had thought of her on this day when he couldn't be there to hold her hand.

The deliverer left, and Lacey admired the gorgeous display of flowers standing on the counter.

"Should I have bought you flowers instead?" Tom asked, flashing an embarrassed side-eye toward his offering of pastries.

"Not at all!" Lacey exclaimed. "The croissants are great as well."

"You can't eat flowers," Gina said through her a mouthful of crumbs. She swallowed and pointed the remaining croissant at Tom like a weapon. "Speaking of eating. When are you making up for cancelling your dinner plans with Lacey? She was so upset over it she turned to drink. And linguine."

Tom looked confused, and Lacey felt her cheeks get hot. She flashed Gina a stern look.

"She's being silly," she explained. "We had a lovely night, with a bottle of wine we shared."

"Then we made a cheesecake and went for a stroll along the beach with the dogs," Gina added with a cackle, waving her croissant around and spewing crumbs on the floor.

"That sounds very romantic," Tom quipped.

"Oh, that reminds me!" Lacey suddenly said, turning to Gina. "I went and explored the island this morning. After your sheep woke me up so rudely, I realized it was low tide and the sandbar was out. Chester and I went over."

Tom's eyebrows shot up. "You went to the island? Did you see the medieval ruins?"

"Only briefly. I didn't want to spend too long there in case the tide came in and trapped me. But from what I did see, it all looked very beautiful."

"Then that's what we should do on our next date," Tom said. "Go and explore the castle. It's best in the moonlight. What do you reckon? You, me, the moonlight, a ruined castle?"

Chester whined.

"And a guard dog," Tom added, crouching down and playfully rubbing Chester either side of his head.

"I mean, that sounds great," Lacey said. "But the sandbar is only out until 7 p.m. at this time of year. If we went over there for the moon, we'd have to stay the whole night." She gasped. "You're not suggesting we go camping, are you?"

Lacey had long suspected Tom was the sort of man who enjoyed hiking in remote wildernesses, pitching a tent, and singing songs around the campfire. Having been born and raised in New York City, Lacey had no proclivity for such activity, nor the desire to partake in it, and she'd been dreading the moment she had to break the news to him.

But Tom was laughing. "No, I'm not suggesting we camp there! I have a fishing boat. I can row us over."

"You have a fishing boat?" Lacey exclaimed.

While it was perfectly fitting with Tom's personality for him to fish and own a rowboat, Lacey was surprised it had never come up in conversation before. While Tom had never been one to toot his own horn, it still seemed odd he'd never mentioned it. Maybe he'd been holding off telling her about it, just like she was with him and her hatred of camping? Maybe they were both trying to hide the bits of themselves that were obviously incompatible with the other...

"Is that a yes, then?" Tom probed. "Shall we go tonight?"

"Okay!" Lacey exclaimed. She was suddenly very excited about the prospect of Tom rowing her across the ocean to explore the medieval ruins with her. But then she remembered she was too busy at the moment. Their schedules just didn't seem to be matching up at the moment.

She deflated. "I can't tonight. I have that meeting with Ivan, about the sale of Crag Cottage."

Gina looked particularly excited about that. She'd been thrilled when Lacey told her she was thinking of making her life as her neighbor on the cliff sides of England permanent.

"We could go after," Tom said. "I'll get everything ready with the boat and you can just let me know when your meeting is over, then come down and meet me on the beach. It could even be a *hey you're buying a house* celebration."

"Only if the meeting goes well," Lacey qualified.

"Which it will," Gina said.

"I guess that could work," Lacey told Tom. Then she nodded. "Let's do it. It's a date."

"Great." He gave her a small peck on the lips. "I'd better let you finish your auction preparations. I'll be back in time for kick off."

Lacey watched him push the now empty trolley back across the cobblestones to his own store, then turned to Gina and flashed her a mock angry glare.

"You are in so much trouble, lady," she said.

Gina gave a cheeky shrug. "Got you your date, didn't I?"

"Hmmm," Lacey said, thinly, not convinced. "Now, I'm going to check everything's ready in the auction room," she told her. "Don't do anything naughty while you're unsupervised."

She went out back to make sure everything was finalized for the auction. It was all looking very nice, Lacey having decked out the room with a nautical theme.

She got to work straightening out the programs on the chairs, when she heard a noise and swirled. A very handsome, Spanish-looking man had wandered in through the doorway. He was dressed in a sharp suit, and his dark hair was coiffed back with gel.

Lacey frowned, and shook her head. Where was Gina? She was supposed to be on the till!

She peered past the man and saw Gina playing games with Boudicca and Chester. She rolled her eyes.

"Excuse me," the man said politely, in a soft Spanish accent. "I'm here for the auction. Am I in the wrong place?"

"Right place," Lacey told him. "Just the wrong time. The auction starts in an hour."

The man looked at his right wrist and sighed. "Of course. There's an hour difference in England. I forgot to change my watch when I got off the plane."

Lacey's curiosity about the man intensified. Had he come from abroad specifically for the auction? Surely not.

He took a further step inside, and the scent of his aftershave brought the hint of a memory with it. Had she seen this man before?

"I came to bid on a Robert Brettell Bate sextant," he said.

Suddenly, Lacey remembered. The man *had* been in her store before, while she'd been attending to the elderly gentleman and the broken ballerina statue. He'd been looking at the naval items, then had disappeared.

She quirked her head to the side, not only out of intrigue, but out of surprise that he actually knew the name of the sextant's maker. Robert Brettell Bate, a nineteenth-century scientific instrument maker, may have been famous in antique collector circles thanks to his role as an optician to the royals, but his existence wasn't exactly known to the average layperson. Which led to only one conclusion; this man was not the average layperson.

"You are selling one today, that's correct?" the man added, presumably in response to her curious expression.

"Yes, that's right."

"I don't suppose we could make an arrangement now?" he asked. "What price are you hoping to fetch?"

Lacey shook her head. "I'm sorry, but the sextant is the main draw. I'd have a lot of disappointed auctioneers if my star item wasn't here," she told him. "You'll just have to come back for the auction to bid on it."

How odd that for the second time she had to turn down a sale! Finding it by chance in the charity shop had been even more of a discovery than she'd realized.

"The auction starts in an hour, you say?" he asked.

"That's right. And it will probably last for about two hours. The sextant will be the final item. I would expect roughly three forty-five will be the time I start the bidding on it."

He shifted from foot to foot as he looked at his watch, seemingly impatient. "Okay. I'll still be able to make my flight if I leave by four." He looked up into Lacey's eyes, his irises the color of cocoa. "I'll see you later."

Lacey watched the mysterious, handsome stranger turn and disappear through the archway.

CHAPTER SIX

The first people to arrive for the auction were the members of the English Antiques Society. They'd gotten a minibus to the store, deciding to make a day trip out of it. As Lacey showed them into the auction room, they cooed and cawed at all the nautical themed decorations and the tea and pastries that were once again on offer.

"You do know how to spoil us," Roger, the society's rosy-cheeked, unofficial spokesman said.

The place began to fill up. Lacey noticed a handful of her London antique dealers enter together, and noticed someone else milling around behind them as if a bit uncertain, with shiny blond dyed hair. It was Brooke from the tearoom.

Lacey went over to her. "Brooke! I wasn't expecting you to come here."

"I wanted to see you in action," the woman told her in her thick Aussie accent. Thanks to the warm weather, she was in a tank top and her large biceps were on display, drawing looks from others in the crowd. "Thought you could do with some support."

"That's really kind of you," Lacey said to her, genuinely touched. Her hopes that Brooke may become an ally in this town grew stronger.

From over Brooke's shoulder, Lacey saw Buck and Daisy come in. Her stomach dropped to her feet and she failed to hold back her grimace.

"What is it?" Brooke asked, sounding concerned. She'd obviously seen the sudden change in Lacey's expression.

"Just some unwelcome visitors."

Brooke looked over her shoulder, then quickly back to Lacey, her eyes now wide. "What the heck are they doing here?"

Lacey sighed. "Daisy saw the sextant through the window and made up her mind she wanted it. But since it's the main auction item, I refused to sell it to her and said if she really wanted it, she'd have to come back today and bid on it like everyone else."

"You called her bluff," Brooke said, in a tone that suggested she thought that had been a very unwise move on Lacey's part.

"I guess I did. And it looks like it's backfired on me."

She watched Buck pace up to the refreshments stand and help himself to croissants as if he were at an all you can eat buffet. Daisy, on the other hand, looked genuinely excited to be here, and was pacing around taking in the decorations. Maybe, like the man with the ballerina figurine, she had a personal connection to the sextant? A family member in the navy, for example.

"I can't imagine Buck responded well to being told no," Brooke continued. "They came to the tearoom again yesterday evening, drunk, and I tried to refuse them service. Well, you can imagine how well that went. In the end, it was easier just to give in rather than stand up to him. Luckily, Buck's a sleepy drunk rather than an aggressive one. I was prepared to use a cactus on him, though, if I had to."

Lacey couldn't help but smile. But it quickly faded at the daunting reality of conducting an auction—her second, nonetheless—in front of the brute of a man.

Brooke reached out and patted Lacey's arm. "You've got this," she said, reassuringly. "Don't let two stubborn Texans spoil this for you." She looked back at Daisy tottering around on her heels, before returning her focus to Lacey. "I mean, look at that woman. What does she actually want with an antique sextant? I bet she can't even spell antique. Or sextant!"

But Lacey no longer wanted to join in with the gossip. People had judged her when she'd been the town's outsider, after all. In fact, people were judging Brooke, right now—embellishing that whole thing about her being a high school wrestler into something more than it was, gawping at her like she was some kind of circus freak just because she'd managed to exercise away her bingo wings. Lacey wasn't going to stoop to those levels.

"You never know," she said, looking over at where Daisy was now towering over the snack table on her six inch stilettos, sniffing the croissants with a disgusted look on her face. "People can surprise you."

Brooke seemed to catch her drift immediately. "You're right." She followed Lacey's gaze. But when she turned back, she was biting her bottom lip to stop from laughing. "Who knows. Maybe she wrote a thesis on nautical sextants?" She immediately held her hands up in truce position. "Sorry! Sorry! That was the last one, I promise. I just couldn't help it!"

Lacey smirked, and Brooke went off to take her seat. Just as she left, Lacey noticed the European stranger she'd been speaking to earlier slip into the auction room quietly and take the closest seat to the door. He sat with his arms resting on his knees, very much like he was ready to spring up and disappear at any second. His posture definitely made him seem like he was in a hurry.

She was about to approach and say hi when her attention was diverted by Tom coming in. He waved, his relaxed body language making the tenseness of the Spanish man even more evident.

Lacey waved back, then noticed the clock had struck one and it was time to begin the auction.

She went up to the pulpit, her heartbeat thrumming in her ears. A hushed silence fell in the room and Lacey cleared her throat.

"Welcome, everyone. It's great to see you all here today. There's some familiar faces in the crowd, and some new ones. I hope everyone finds something they're looking for today in this treasure trove of nautical themed delights. Speaking of treasure, let me introduce to you the first piece in today's repertoire. A naval lapel pin. This is genuine 1910, First World War memorabilia. I'd like to start the bidding at forty."

And with that, Lacey was away, working through the items one by one. A collection of bronze telescopes went for just over two hundred pounds. The anchor of a decommissioned naval vessel fetched almost a thousand. But the big money maker was still to come. The sextant.

Any hope that Buck and Daisy would get bored and leave disappeared as she went. They sat there, the whole time, letting each item pass them by. They really were that stubborn.

Lacey couldn't help but notice that the Spanish man was doing the same thing. He was obviously uninterested in anything else she was selling. He sat through the whole auction, waiting for just one thing.

"Now, this is a very special item coming up next," Lacey announced. "And all the proceeds from its sale will be given to the charity shop I found it in. This is a real, genuine antique Robert Brettell Bate sextant, in perfect condition. This is the highly sought after double-framed design, with a genuine ivory handle, and original mahogany wood case. I'll start the bidding at one thousand pounds."

Buck jumped up. "Here!" he bellowed.

His voice was so loud, everyone in the seats around him flinched. Lacey noticed people glancing back over their shoulders warily.

"One thousand pounds to the gentleman in the cowboy hat," Lacey said. "Can I get one thousand one hundred?"

With calm determination, the Spanish stranger stretched up his hand.

Lacey accepted his bid and raised the asking price by another hundred. Buck was up and out of his seat in a flash, waving his fist in the air.

Lacey felt her heart rate spike with every hundred that went back and forth between the two men. Not out of excitement for the huge sum of money the sextant was drawing in for charity, but because Buck's face was getting increasingly more red each time he was outbid. He looked like he was about to explode.

But the Spanish man wasn't backing down yet. In complete contrast to Buck, he remained entirely expressionless.

As the price continued rising up and up and up, beads of sweat started to roll down Buck's forehead. But he obviously wasn't about to be outbid, especially not with Daisy in the seat beside him egging him on.

But the stranger also appeared to have bottomless pockets. Unlike Buck, whose face was going quite red with every thousand pounds added to the price, the stranger looked serene.

"Two thousand five hundred?" Lacey said, turning to Buck.

He paused. It was obvious to Lacey that he wanted to stop.

He was tomato-red now, and tugging at the collar of his shirt as if to get more air. Then Daisy prodded him, and just like that, his hand went right up into the air.

Far from the man who'd bossed his wife around before, Buck now seemed completely under her command.

"Two thousand six hundred," Lacey said, looking toward the stranger.

To her surprise, he shook his head.

Momentarily taken aback that a man who had apparently flown to England from Spain specifically for this auction had seemingly given up, Lacey almost forgot what she was doing. But she snapped back to the moment, and banged the gavel.

Sold. After all that, the antique sextant was going to Buck and Daisy.

Buck leapt up and punched the air, like he'd just heard he'd won a bet on the boxing. Daisy squealed and clapped her hands with excitement. The whole display was very uncouth, and Lacey could see pretty much every single person in the audience bristle in irritation. Those amongst the audience who owned stores in Wilfordshire—who, presumably, had had their own run-ins with the infuriating pair—couldn't stop themselves from glaring darkly at the two of them and their hooping, hollering, distasteful display of triumph. Lacey had to remind herself that the money was going to charity, even if the rare item was going home with *them*.

"That's it, folks. Thank you so much for attending today. If all winners would like to come with me to sort out payments."

She hopped down from the pulpit and looked over at the exit, noticing that the Spanish man had already gone. He must have slipped out immediately after losing out on the bidding, off to catch his flight home. She wondered why he'd given up on the item that had lured him from overseas. She doubted it was money related; there were usually signs on people's faces when they were reaching their limit, or pushing too far, like Buck's sweating face and shirt-tugging. But the Spanish man had looked calm the whole way through until he'd unexpectedly bowed out. It was all rather curious.

Lacey went behind her desk and began the arduous task of dealing with all the administrative work—signing certificates of ownership, taking down payments, and scheduling shipments. It was all going smoothly enough, until Buck muscled his way to the front of the queue.

"Don't worry about any of that unnecessary paperwork," he said. "I'll take my prize now."

Prize, Lacey thought with distaste, *As if the auction was a competition he'd won.*

He reminded Lacey of Benjamin Archer, who'd demanded he take the grandfather clock with him the moment it had sold.

"I'm afraid it doesn't quite work like that," Lacey explained. "We take a ten percent card payment now and then on successful delivery of the item, the rest of the money is collected from the card."

"Are you really still telling me my money isn't good enough for you?" Buck snapped. "You think I can't pay you?"

"Not at all," Lacey explained. "It's to protect everyone involved, you and I both. What if the item isn't to your liking once it's delivered to you?"

"I don't need it delivered to me. I can put it in my bag and take it away right now."

"Now come on, chap," Roger from the English Antiques Society said, jumping to her defense. "It needs to be packaged properly and delivered. It is standard practice."

"You shut it, old man," Buck said. He looked back at Lacey, glaring darkly. "When Buckland Stringer says he's going to do something, then he's going to do it! And some stupid little girl isn't going to stop me!"

His six-foot frame seemed suddenly to grow to eight foot, as he thumped his fists on the desk and loomed over Lacey.

"Hey!" Brooke exclaimed, marching over to Lacey's side. "Back the hell off!"

Lacey raised her hands. She wanted this altercation over with right now.

"Sir, you can take the item today but I'll need to take the payment in full and have you sign a waiver."

Buck looked superior. "See. That wasn't so hard, was it? A bit of compromise. I'll wire you the money. It'll take a couple of days."

"That's not what she said!" Brooke snapped, squaring up again.

Lacey leapt in. "Okay. Fine. Whatever. Just take it."

She was reluctant, but the last thing she wanted was for a fight to break out in a store filled with delicate antiques. With his huge frame and angry demeanor Buck would, quite literally, be a bull in a china shop.

As soon as he was gone, Brooke turned to Lacey.

"Sorry. I didn't mean to make anything worse there. I just can't stand by while men bully and intimidate women, you know?" She shuddered. "My ex-hubby was like that. Always demanding his own way. Maybe that's why I mock Daisy so much. I see something of myself in her, scurrying around after her fella while he ruins everyone's day, relieved that for the time being, he's taking it out on someone else and not you."

Lacey could see the sorrow in Brooke's eyes as she reminisced about her painful past. It seemed so strange to her. She couldn't quite picture this woman, who seemed so bubbly and confident, being cowed by a bully of a husband.

Perhaps she'd learned to act that way as a defense strategy, as a way to ward off bad memories.

Lacey sighed. It really wasn't how she'd wanted the day to end, and with Brooke's glumness thrown into the mix as well, she was feeling thoroughly bummed out.

But then her phone pinged with a message. Ivan had sent her a text. She checked it.

Still meeting tonight?

At the thought of owning Crag Cottage, Lacey's mood instantly lifted.

You bet, she texted back.

Then she smiled and reminded herself that the Bucks of the world were there to make the good moments even sweeter.

The fight with Buck was still fresh in Lacey's mind as she twisted her Rapunzel key in the lock of Crag Cottage. It had been a difficult day, filled with ups and downs, and she was a bit bitter it had ended on such a sour note. Buck had been very aggressive, and she didn't even know if she'd ever get any money for the sextant. The fact that it was a charity who'd miss out if Mr. Nasty Loudmouth didn't cough up made it even worse.

She'd just had time to change out of her work clothes when she heard the familiar rat-a-tat-tat on her door of Ivan. He always knocked the same way; tentatively, as if he didn't want to intrude, even though he was invited and most welcome!

Lacey put all thoughts of the fight from her mind and trotted down the steps.

When she opened the door, she found that Ivan had not come alone. Standing on the doorstep was a smartly dressed woman.

"Oh," Lacey said, surprised. "I didn't realize your wife was coming."

The woman shook her head. "I'm not Ivan's wife. I'm a property lawyer. Michelle Braithwaite."

She held out her hand.

Lacey looked at the woman, confused as to why a lawyer was present. She shook the hand being offered to her.

"Come inside," she said, gesturing them in. "The kitchen's this way."

As they strolled along the darkened hallway toward the bright light of the kitchen at the other end, Lacey flashed a curious expression at Ivan.

"You brought a lawyer?" she asked him out of the corner of her mouth. "Should I be worried?"

"Not at all," Ivan replied. All Lacey could really see of him were his teeth, which were glowing in the beam of light coming from the kitchen. He was grinning.

They entered the kitchen and Lacey offered drinks. Ivan, for the first time ever, accepted a beer. Michelle politely declined. She had the efficient quality all lawyers seemed to possess.

They all took a seat at the butcher's block table, then Michelle took some papers from her bag.

"This is all the paperwork here," she announced.

"The paperwork for..."

"The house!" Ivan exclaimed, clearly too excited to hold it back anymore. "These are the deeds to transfer ownership to you."

Lacey was taken aback. This meeting was meant to be about working out the finer details of the deal, but it seemed as if they'd already been decided without her?

"Ivan, I can sign deeds to the house without putting all the financial things in place."

"Those are included," Michelle said, tapping the top of the stack of papers.

"No offense," Lacey said, "but doesn't the bank need to be involved with those?"

She was worried Ivan had paid some rogue lawyer to draw up a contract that would satisfy no one and leave them both vulnerable. He could easily be taken advantage of, and Lacey was concerned this was one of these occasions.

She looked over at him. "We were supposed to discuss all this first."

"What's to discuss?" he said haplessly. "This suits us both."

Lacey let out a deep sigh. It had been hasty of her to expect this meeting to go without a hitch. Of course it had to go wrong. Like Buck and Daisy at the auction, this rogue lawyer was intruding on another important moment in her life and ruining it.

"What if I'm not happy with the arrangements?"

"You will be," Ivan said, confidently, tapping the paper. "Just have a read."

Lacey did just that. And what she saw made her jaw drop open. Not because the deal was bad, but because it was actually very, very good!

The contract stipulated that Lacey could pay in installments, thus bypassing the need for a bank loan, saving them both bank fees and stamp duties and all the other things that would have to be paid if they'd done this through an estate agent.

"What do you think?" Ivan asked, back to his usual uncertain self. "Is it okay?"

It was more than okay. Lacey was over the moon. They'd save a fortune completing the sale privately, and the contract was just to protect them both in the unlikely event that something went wrong along the way!

"Um, yes, it's perfect," Lacey said. "Unless you've hidden some small print somewhere? Do I have to give you my firstborn child, or sacrifice a goat or something?"

Ivan laughed. Michelle didn't.

"I can assure you there's no small print," she said. "But of course, take your time reading everything through. There's no rush. When you're ready to sign, let me know and we can arrange to meet with witnesses."

She stood, and clipped her brief case closed.

Lacey stood too, shocked the meeting was ending so abruptly.

"I mean, I probably don't need time, but I should at least sleep on it," Lacey said. Her heart was pulling her in one direction, her mind telling her to slow down just a little bit.

Michelle was already heading for the door. Lacey looked at Ivan and he shrugged. She hurried after Michelle and saw her out.

"She was in a rush," Lacey said as they watched her drive away.

"She's in high demand," Ivan said.

"I can see why. That's one hell of a contract she's devised. Are you sure you want to do it this way?"

While circumnavigating the usual process of buying and selling property would save them both money, it did leave them vulnerable. A relationship breakdown, for example. Lacey thought of her late alimony payment to David, which had been beyond her control and yet could easily have landed her in some hot water. If a similar thing happened with one of her installments, it could damage

Ivan's trust in her. There was no middleman. No cushion. No bank that could repossess the house if it fell into debt. It would just be hers, like that, with the promise of paying Ivan's installments.

"I'm certain," Ivan said. "You're already doing me a huge favor taking it off my hands. The holiday cottages are filling up quickly as we approach summer and I just don't have the time to be worrying about this place. Honestly, the quicker we get this done and dusted, the better for us both. Unless you're not sure you want to settle here anymore? I don't want to make you feel like you have to if you've changed your mind and—"

Lacey squeezed his arm, interrupting him mid anxious monologue. "I want it. That's not in question. I just want to make sure we're both protected. This deal relies on a fair bit of trust."

"I have trust in you," Ivan said.

He left, the meeting ending far sooner than Lacey had imagined, and having gone better than she could've ever dreamed.

Feeling like she was walking on cloud nine, Lacey sent Tom a message explaining that the meeting was over and she was heading down to the beach with Chester. She couldn't wait to tell him about the deeds face to face.

She headed out the back door, grabbing Chester's leash from the hook where it was hanging, and went across the lawn to the hidden cliff steps she'd discovered. Chester went on ahead, hopping down the crude steps cut into the cliff face with the elegance of an ibex. She went down after him.

On the beach, there was no sign of Tom, but Lacey wasn't surprised; it was far earlier than either of them had anticipated, after all. In fact, the meeting with Ivan had ended so quickly, there was still a small sliver of sandbar out, a strip of bridge linking the beach to the island.

At that exact same moment Lacey decided she'd better put Chester on his leash, the dog went racing across the beach, heading straight for the sandbar.

"Chester!" Lacey bellowed, pulling the leash from her pocket and racing after him. "Stop!"

Uncharacteristically for her usually obedient dog, Chester ignored her command.

He was so much faster than her, and quickly became a little spot in the distance. It was like he was on a mission!

Lacey reached the sandbar, panting, and looked at the sliver of sand with water lapping up either side of it. The ocean was ready to consume the path at any moment, but Lacey hated the idea of being separated from Chester.

She swallowed her nerves and hurried after him.

Her shoes were soaked by the time she made it to the other side.

"Chester!" she cried, calling out to the dog once she'd reached the island. "Where are you?"

She could hear him scrabbling around, sniffing and barking. The noise was coming from the other side of a small patch of trees.

She went through.

"There you are!" she said, emerging through the thicket to see Chester standing on the beach beside a large, dark object.

But as Lacey drew closer, she gasped.

It wasn't an object. It was a person. A person lying face down in the surf.

Lacey raced over, dropping to her knees beside them. She reached, taking them by the shoulders, and turning them over. She found herself staring into the eyes of Buckland Stringer.

The man was dead.

CHAPTER SEVEN

Lacey leapt back like she'd touched flame, and landed on her backside in the sand. She couldn't believe what she was seeing. A dead body!

Another dead body.

Feeling burning bile rise in her throat, Lacey tried to scrabble backward. But she was so disoriented from shock, her sodden shoes seemed unable to find purchase, and she ended up kicking sand onto Buck's bulky chest.

'*Stop!*' she scolded herself, as the horrible reality began to sink in that she had, once again, stumbled upon a crime scene.

Although . . . perhaps not?

With morbid curiosity, Lacey noticed that Buck showed no obvious signs of having met foul play. Maybe he'd died a natural death? A heart attack, perhaps? He'd had a penchant for steaks and angry outbursts, after all. They were probably the two biggest contributors to poor heart health.

As she stared at his pale, bloodless face, unable to look away, Lacey found herself silently praying the man had succumbed to a natural death. But some instinct inside of her told her that this just wasn't the case. His expression was surprised, as if he'd had no warning his final moment was coming.

Then there was the sand . . .

His mouth and nose was covered in it, as if someone had shoved his face into the sand to suffocate him.

There was no denying it. Buck had been murdered.

Lacey turned her face and vomited onto the sand. Chester barked, becoming even more agitated by the sight of his mistress heaving than he'd already been by the presence of a dead body.

"I'm okay," Lacey assured him, wiping the acid from her lips with the back of her hand. "Don't worry, Chester."

The dog whinnied sadly and nudged her.

Suddenly, coming from somewhere behind her, Lacey heard the sound of footsteps thudding against wet sand. She wasn't alone. And whoever else it was on the island, they were coming right for her.

Her coordination came back in a split second as her ancient instincts of fight or flight kicked in. She leaped up so fast, black spots flashed in her eyes.

"STAY BACK!" she screamed, jutting her hand forward, palm up, in a "*Stop Mr. Postman*" dance move. As if she could in any way ward off an attacker with just her hand, Lacey thought, chastising herself, before quickly adding, "MY DOG WILL BITE YOU!"

"Lacey?" a male voice replied. "What the heck is going on?"

The black stars disappeared from her eyes and Lacey saw that the figure emerging before her was not a murderer at all, but Tom.

Tom!

He rushed toward her, his expression turning to utter panic.

The freeze response released its hold on Lacey and she practically fell into him, burying her face against his broad chest, breathing in the familiar, comforting smell of freshly baked pastry.

"Oh Tom," she whimpered, as she trembled in his arms. "Tom, it's Buck. He's . . . he's dead."

She felt a sudden hitch in Tom's chest, then the tightness of his arms around her loosened as he went to see for himself.

Now that her fixation on the cadaver had finally been broken, Lacey couldn't bear to turn back and look at it another time. She kept her eyes averted, even when she heard the sharp intake of Tom's breath that told her he'd now seen the body.

"What . . ." Tom said, the word sounding as if it had been pulled out of his lungs involuntarily. "What happened?" He took her by the shoulders, searching her eyes. "Did he hurt you?"

Lacey wrenched herself free.

"I didn't do this!" she exclaimed, stung by the insinuation that she'd been responsible for Buck's death. "He was like this when I found him!"

Tom hesitated. His words came out in flustered stammers. "Right. Sorry. Yes. Of course."

But there was no back tracking. The damage was done.

Lacey reeled. How could Tom even think for a second that she could have done such a thing? Beyond the fact Buck had at least a foot and a hundred pounds on her small feminine frame and killing him would have been physically impossible for her to do, there was the small fact that she was not a murderer!

"I can't believe you thought I killed him..." Lacey said, pacing away from her beau.

The comfort Tom's presence had brought to the scene before seemed to suddenly disappear. Now she wanted him gone. She wanted distance.

She crossed her arms and tightened them around her middle.

Tom paced toward her with an outstretched hand. "I'm sorry, Lace. I didn't mean—"

"Don't call me that," Lacey snapped.

"What?" Tom asked.

He was frowning now. Confused. Unsure what he'd done wrong or how to put it right, Lacey thought. And he couldn't put it right. There was no way for him to take back what he'd said, or the fact he'd entertained the thought she could be capable of murder, no matter how brief.

"It's what David called me," she said. "Lace. I don't like it."

It was the first time Lacey had realized she didn't like the pet name. And now was obviously *not* the time to be bringing it up, but the stress of the moment had made her speak before thinking.

"Oh," Tom replied.

Lacey noticed the dejection in his face; the downturn at the side of his lips that she'd never seen before.

She lowered herself down onto a boulder. Chester rushed over, nuzzling his nose into her lap. She stroked him, hypnotically, the feel of his fur beneath her fingers barely registering.

She stared out at the ocean. The sky had turned gray, like a watercolor painting, and the ocean beneath it was flat, barely moving. A cold breeze stirred at the base of her neck, making Lacey aware that she'd been perspiring.

"We should call the police," Tom said, his voice sounding like it was a million miles away.

Lacey thought of Detective Superintendent Turner. Detective Constable Inspector Lewis. She'd fought so hard to clear her name with them, and now she was about to be thrust into that nightmare all over again.

She kept her gaze out to sea as she nodded. Her voice came out monotone with defeat. "Yes. We should."

They arrived by motorized dinghy boat. A whole squad of professionals. Police officers. Crime scene investigators in hazmat suits. Paramedics, who, on realizing they'd be no help at all to Buck, turned their attention to Lacey, declaring her to be in shock, and covering her in one of those silver foil blankets she'd only ever seen on cops shows.

The whole thing felt so surreal. Lacey seemed unable to rise from her boulder, so she sat there, looking out to sea like a siren, while a white tent went up around the body and yellow and blue striped police tape was looped from tree to tree, while crime scene investigators walked around in white suits like they were dealing with an alien invasion rather than a deceased man. She sat there while Tom answered the detectives' questions.

Superintendent Turner had wanted to speak to her first, obviously, but the paramedics had declared she was not yet in a fit state and turned him away. But Lacey knew her turn would come eventually, and she kept catching Superintendent Turner looking over at her suspiciously while Tom was speaking. It was very clear they were far more interested in what she had to say than anything Tom did. She'd found the body, after all. That made her suspect number one.

Just then, she noticed a change in the body language of the detectives. They were finished with Tom now, and were thanking him for his time. There was no more avoiding it. It was her turn.

She tried to keep her breath steady as the two detectives approached.

"Lacey?" Beth Lewis began, flashing her badge. "You remember us, right? I'm DCI Lewis. This is—"

"Superintendent Turner," Lacey finished for her, looking the man directly in the eye. "Yes. I remember you well. How are you, Karl?"

The man blinked, but didn't acknowledge her question. He pointed over to Tom. "I understand from Mr. Forrester you were the first to discover the body."

"That's right," Lacey replied. "Well, Chester found him first, really."

Superintendent Turner's jaw twitched, and he looked down at Chester, obviously displeased. "Ah, yes. Your trusty canine companion. How could I forget dear Fido?"

Chester growled.

DCI Lewis side-eyed her superior and, wisely in Lacey's opinion, interjected before he could say anything else derisory.

"Can you tell me what you were doing on the island?" she asked.

"I came to see the ruins," Lacey said, pointing at the now black silhouette of the medieval castle she'd still not had a chance to explore.

DCI Lewis nodded as she jotted down Lacey's words in her notepad.

"You had plans with Mr. Forrester?" Beth Lewis continued.

Lacey noted the precise way she selected her words, always leading but always vague enough to catch out any discrepancies. Plans could mean anything, after all. One can plan to stroll romantically along the beach hand in hand just as well as one can plan to murder.

"We were going to explore the ruins together under the moonlight," Lacey said confidently. "It was a date."

She watched as DCI Lewis's pen swirled across the paper.

"And where had you arranged to meet Mr. Forrester?" Beth Lewis asked, her gaze flicking up from the notepad to Lacey.

There'd been a shift, Lacey noted, in the detective's gaze. It was a little piercing. Somewhat distrustful. Lacey felt the change.

So this was it. The moment they thought they may catch her in a lie. Because she'd obviously arranged to meet Tom on the beach. And yet she'd then come to the island without him. Didn't that look suspicious?

"The beach," Lacey replied, pointing across the ocean, to the blinking lights of Wilfordshire.

"The plan changed?"

"Chester ran across the sandbar. I went after him."

"What about his lead?" Superintendent Turner interjected. He was looking down at where Chester's leather leash was dragging in the sand.

"He wasn't wearing it before," Lacey explained.

"Does he usually walk around without a lead? What if he runs off?"

"He doesn't. Usually. Or if he does, he responds to my command to stop."

"Not this time, though? This time he ran off and ignored your calls? I always got the impression your dog was obedient."

Lacey paused. This was going too far, now. The detective's questions had already veered from information gathering to judgment making, and she was not going to engage with it anymore.

"Is Chester a suspect, Superintendent Turner?" Lacey asked, coldly. "Or are you just generally curious? I have a great book about dog behavior if you'd like to borrow it."

As was the man's way, he ignored her, and steered the conversation in his desired direction.

"How were you planning on meeting up with Mr. Forrester if you weren't in the prearranged place?"

"I have a phone," came Lacey's blunt reply. "I was going to message him once I'd gotten Chester back."

Superintendent Turner folded his arms and cast Lacey a look of skepticism. But before he had time to ask the inevitable question—"can I see your phone?"—one of the police officers appeared at the tree lines and waved an arm over his head.

"Karl! I need you over here!"

The superintendent gave Lacey once last look. "Don't go anywhere, Miss Doyle."

He paced away, toward the officer flagging him down. DCI Lewis thanked Lacey, snapped her notebook shut, and followed.

Lacey watched them climb the rugged banks toward the trees through which she'd run while chasing after Chester. They must've found something. Some potential piece of evidence. Hopefully, Lacey thought, something that would exonerate her flat out.

She watched all the hubbub taking place over by the trees. Then suddenly Tom was next to her.

His appearance took her by surprise and she flinched.

"Did they say we could talk to one another?" she asked.

Tom responded with a confused frown. "Why wouldn't we be allowed to talk to one another?"

"Usually they keep suspects apart so they can't confer with one another and get their stories straight. Are you sure you can talk to me? I don't want to give them any ammunition."

"We're witnesses, Lacey, not suspects," Tom stated. "They have our statements now anyway."

Lacey raised an eyebrow, unconvinced. "Witnesses?" she repeated, tonelessly.

Tom looked perplexed. "Lacey, I know you've had a fright and everything but are you okay? You're acting kind of paranoid."

"Can you blame me?" Lacey said. "The same detectives who tried to blame a murder on me before are investigating another that I'm linked to. I mean, even *you* had your doubts about me..."

Tom held up his hand to stop her. It was the same *Mr. Postman* gesture Lacey had used to ward him off when she thought he might be an attacker.

"Lacey, please," he said, sounding more forceful than she'd heard from him before. "I already said I was sorry about that. It just slipped out. I know you didn't do anything. That you'd never do anything like that. My mind just conjured a scenario to fit everything it was seeing into a picture that made sense, and it came up with the wrong thing. That's all."

Lacey let his words hang in the air between them. She could hear the logic in what Tom was saying, and yet the emotional impact of his earlier accusation had struck her so hard it felt like nothing would ever make it stop hurting.

"Let's go home," Tom added, with a pleading edge to his voice. "I know the date's been ruined but we could still just hang out. Be together. I have the boat so I can row us both back to shore."

Lacey paused, her mind latching onto something Tom had said.

"You have the boat?" she repeated.

"Yes. I rowed it here. How else would I have gotten here?"

"The sandbar was out." She spoke flatly, not even sure what she herself was implying.

"Barely," Tom explained. "If I'd walked over here, we'd have had no way to get back to shore. What does it matter anyway?"

"Because we weren't supposed to be meeting here," Lacey told him. "On the island. We were supposed to be meeting on that side of the beach." She pointed across the vast, black ocean. "That was the plan. So why did you row here? It wasn't for me. You had no way of knowing I'd already crossed."

Now it was Tom's turn to look stung. "What are you suggesting?"

"I'm not suggesting anything. I'm asking a question."

It was getting tense between them. Lacey could feel the discomfort increasing.

"You're asking me why I rowed over here?" He ran his hand through his hair. "Dammit, Lacey. Didn't it cross your mind that after you messaged me to say you were leaving the meeting with Ivan early that you'd get to the beach well before me and decide to cross the sandbar on foot?"

But Lacey was shaking her head. The explanation was inadequate. There were gaps in it. Holes.

"You were already here. It must take way longer to row here than it took me to run across the sandbar. So you were already on the island."

Just then, a hubbub erupted from the huddle of officers who'd been around the trees. The commanding voice of Karl Turner boomed out. "Let's get those two out of here."

An officer immediately began to jog toward them.

"We need to escort you off the island," he said, gesturing to the dinghy.

"What about my boat?" Tom said.

"It'll have to stay here for now," the officer replied. "It may be part of the crime scene. We might need to take it in for evidence."

Tom looked over at Lacey, the color draining from his face. It seemed that he'd finally caught up to the reality of the situation; that the pair of them looked extremely suspicious, that their actions that evening, no matter how innocent, had linked them inextricably to a murder investigation.

Without saying a word, they clambered aboard the dingy, Chester hopping to get over the rubber edges. The officer started the boat's engine, and it buzzed like a hornet. Then the boat pulled away, cutting across the flat ocean.

Lacey watched the island shrink, more than acutely aware that what she had seen upon it would change her life forever.

CHAPTER EIGHT

It no longer felt like spring when Lacey awoke the next morning. The empty side of her bed felt colder than normal, knowing that Tom was supposed to be occupying it.

Lacey heaved her body out of bed, disturbing Chester in the process, who sprang up ready to start the day. Lacey, on the other hand, felt heavy. Weary. Like all the good things about yesterday—the meeting with Ivan, the auction—had never really happened, and that everything had always felt dreary and filled with doom.

She dressed without much care, pulling her hair into a low ponytail, and headed downstairs. Despite her fatigue, the thought of drinking coffee made her feel nauseous. In fact, the idea of putting anything in her body after what she'd seen yesterday made her stomach turn.

"Let's just go," she told Chester. "No point hanging around."

She fetched his leash from the hook. He looked at her quizzically. It wasn't usual for her to put him on a leash in the morning, and he was perceptive enough to notice the change in routine.

"Sorry, boy," she told him. "You got me into way too much trouble last time by not wearing this thing. I'm not risking it again. You're staying right by my side."

She clipped the leash on, and they headed out the back door.

Since she'd skipped breakfast and left earlier than normal, Lacey decided to take the longer beach route into town; partly because it was far more tranquil to walk beside the ocean than along the cliff path, where she'd have to squish up onto the verge to allow cars to pass by, but also out of morbid curiosity. Lacey wanted to see what was going on at the island.

She reached the bottom of the cliff steps that led from her garden and headed eastward a few paces, squinting to see across the water. Her eyes scanned the horizon, seeing there was plenty of police activity still going on. They must've been there all night, a team of people prodding and probing an abandoned island for clues. At least two more police vessels had moored up—big metallic ones the size of fishing trawlers, with the police insignia emblazoned across the side, far more intimidating than the dinghy the first had arrived in. Bright police tape was visible even from this distance.

"Everyone will know," Lacey said to no one in particular.

She took a deep breath and turned back the way she'd come, beginning the trek toward town.

Now she knew that the police activity was more than visible from the shore, she knew that every single person in Wilfordshire would know something was going on. Perhaps not the specifics, but two huge trawlers and bright police tape were not usual goings-on and the whispers would have started. Lacey braced herself.

The long route always took her to the wrong side of the high street, the end opposite where her store was located, and to the corner where the Coach House Inn stood. Getting past there would be her first challenge. The pub was a hotbed for gossip.

Luckily, it wasn't open for business yet.

But just as she was celebrating her good fortune, Lacey spotted Brenda the bartender trying to shoo seagulls off the picnic benches outside. By the looks of things, the tables had been used after closing time by a group of people eating fries and drinking shop-bought canned beer, because the detritus from their gathering lay strewn all over the place. Brenda was looking understandably pissed about it, which Lacey could fully appreciate. If she had picnic benches outside the store that got messed up overnight by people who weren't even customers, bringing a bunch of notoriously aggressive birds with them, she'd be pretty annoyed too.

She tried to pass quickly, but Brenda spotted her and looked up.

"Lacey!" she exclaimed, dropping her arms and abandoning her attempts to shoo the seagulls. "Did you hear what happened?"

Lacey paused. She felt her stomach clench. Brenda had never been chatty with her before. She couldn't help but feel suspicious of her.

"Morning," she called, trying to play it off as if she'd not heard the question.

But the girl paced over. "You've not heard, have you?" she said. "Lacey, there's been a *murder!*"

Lacey had no choice. She had to stop walking. And she had to be honest. When it came out that she'd been the one to find the body—and it *would* come out, Lacey was sure of that—then pretending not to know now anything would come back to bite her in the ass.

She nodded slowly. "Yes. I heard."

"Do you know who it is?" Brenda asked, in a tone that implied she did but was testing Lacey's knowledge. She sounded almost like a school child on the playground, her tone a mixture of excitement and terror.

"Buck," Lacey said. "The American tourist."

Brenda nodded. "Yeah! Can you believe it? He was murdered! Out on the island!"

Lacey tightened her arms against her chest. That was some pretty specific and accurate information. She wondered whether Brenda's source was an officer.

"Gruesome," Lacey replied vaguely.

Brenda nodded again. She looked like a wide-eyed child, half disturbed but half enthralled. "You know," she said, lowering her voice, "I don't think he'll be missed around these parts. Him and that wife of his have been pissing off folk left, right and center. You know he slapped my arse the other night? Right in front of his wife. She just laughed like it was some kind of joke, but the joke was on them, because my fella was sat at the bar visiting me during my shift. He went ballistic. You should've seen him! Barry had to step in. He kicked Buck and Daisy out and threatened to ban my Ed if he ever did anything like that again!"

Lacey listened attentively. She knew Ed even more tangentially than she knew Brenda, but she knew he was a bit of a tough guy, the type who walked with a swagger and showed off his gym honed physique in black T-shirts. Could Brenda's boyfriend have gotten his revenge on Buck? Evened the score for disrespecting his girlfriend? He could definitely match him physically, and had already had one altercation with the man.

Lacey filed her suspicions away in her mind.

The seagulls that had been pestering the pub before were back, and Lacey decided to use them as an out.

"Looks like you have some unwanted visitors."

The blond girl looked over her shoulder, then huffed loudly. "Ah. I'd better sort them out." She turned and hurried away, but called as she went, "Watch your back, yeah? There's a murderer on the loose."

73

Lacey shivered at the thought and left.

As she strode along the cobblestones, the bunting that criss-crossed the street seemed too bright and cheerful now considering the circumstances. The spring bulbs in the planters that dotted the road seemed equally incongruous. Mocking, almost. Buck's life had been taken from him at a time when the whole town was celebrating new life.

Just then, Lacey noticed her next hurdle. The toy shop was coming up on her righthand side, and standing in the doorway, sipping coffee from a mug, stood Jane, the store's owner. Jane was another local business owner who always seemed to have her finger on the pulse and her ear to the ground, knowing everyone's business.

Lacey felt herself tense up, knowing that the second Jane spotted her it would be game over. How many more of these interruptions was she going to have to endure before she reached the safety of her store? Was she going to be forced to drag up those images and memories every foot along the high street? Was every store clerk going to want to engage in conversation about the horrible murder? Despite its many positives, the small-town gossipdom that ruled Wilfordshire was not to Lacey's taste. She'd grown up with the blank impersonality of New York City, after all.

"Lacey!" Jane called, waving.

The last thing Lacey wanted to do was go over, so she tried to keep walking, giving Jane a cursory yet noncommittal wave.

"Did you hear about Buck?" Jane called loudly.

Lacey tensed, but didn't slow her step. "Grim business, huh?"

"Did the police speak to you yet?" Jane called.

Well, there was no getting out of it now. Lacey stopped in her tracks. She knew it would look worse in everyone's eyes if she appeared to be hiding anything, and so she accepted her fate and turned her full attention to the toy shop owner.

Jane had the friendly demeanor of a preschool teacher, but she'd been right in there accusing Lacey with the rest of them when Iris had been murdered. Lacey didn't quite know whether she could trust her or not. But if Jane had reason to think Lacey had spoken to the police already, then perhaps even more gossip had filtered to the locals than Lacey had anticipated. Because, although she'd been the first on scene, and therefore spoken to the police immediately, there was no reason for Jane to assume as much. Someone must've told her.

"Yes," Lacey said, taking a few tentative steps toward the woman. "Why do you ask?"

Jane took a sip of coffee. Her right shoulder was butted up against the door frame, in a position that seemed too languorous considering the heaviness of the topic they were discussing.

"Because of the sextant," she said.

The mismatch between Jane's tone and expression was not lost on Lacey. She'd said her statement innocently enough, but there was a hardness in her eyes, that seemed to be pinning Lacey to the spot. Judging her. And the small twitch between the woman's eyebrows was enough to tell Lacey she was suspicious of her.

"The sextant?" Lacey asked. "What's that got to do with anything?"

"Buck bought it in your auction, didn't he?" Jane asked, failing to fully maintain the tone of fake innocence, and starting to sound slightly accusatory. "And demanded to take it with him?"

Lacey immediately picked up on Jane's tactic. She was deflecting Lacey's question with one of her own. It was the same thing Superintendent Turner always did, the thing that infuriated her. A swirling pit of dread opened up in her stomach as it became more and more apparent that Jane suspected her of having something to do with Buck's murder.

"Yes..." Lacey said, her mouth now bone dry. "And why does that matter?"

"Because Daisy told the police the sextant was stolen from their hotel room." She eyed Lacey in a way that suggested she was searching for a reaction. "The police reckon Buck was killed over it."

Involuntarily, Lacey felt her hand fly up to her mouth. A million thoughts came to the forefront of her mind. Could Buck really have been killed over an antique? An antique she'd been the initial proprietor of? And if what Jane was saying was true, where did it put her in the picture? Surely it gave the police even more reason to suspect her!

"There was a man," Lacey stammered, speaking before her brain had had the chance to fully engage.

"A man?" Jane asked. Any attempts on her part to conceal her true curiosity had failed. She studied Lacey like she was a museum artifact.

Lacey shook her head, something in the back of her brain telling her not to speak to Jane of all people about any of this. But the Spanish man had popped back into her mind's eye, his image crystal clear and pristine. He'd been bidding on the sextant. He'd dropped out of the race without even a hint of emotion. Could he have been the one to do this?

"Lacey?" Jane asked.

Lacey snapped back to the moment. "I have to go. Sorry."

She hurried away, stumbling over the uneven cobbles in her haste. Her desire to get inside her store was more imperative than ever.

It was barely ten feet from her when she slammed right into her next hurdle. Someone had stepped directly in front of her.

"Lacey," a male voice said. "I was just coming to see you."

"Stephen?" Lacey said, drawing back and looking into the eyes of the man who leased her the store. "You were? Is everything okay?"

"With me? Yes. It's you I'm worried about."

Just then, Lacey noticed Taryn had come to the door of her boutique, and was watching her like a hawk.

"Why are you worried about me?" Lacey asked Stephen, her eyes scanning around for some kind of excuse to escape.

Stephen lowered his voice. "I heard about the murder. Of Buck, the man who'd just bought something from your auction. And that the item was stolen from his hotel room. And that the police think that was the motive?"

The swirling in Lacey's mind worsened. She felt like she was going to pass out. Taryn's eyes seemed to be burning holes in the back of her skull and into her brain, which was now throbbing.

"I..." Lacey said, opening her mouth, then closing it again without formulating a full sentence.

Stephen took her by the shoulders and looked intently into her eyes.

"It's alright," he told her, firmly. "No one suspects you! Goodness, Lacey. Is that what you were thinking?"

He laughed, and the noise was too loud for Lacey's frayed nerves to handle.

"You don't?" she asked.

"Of course not!" Stephen exclaimed. "It's always the partner, isn't it? Nine times out of ten it's a lovers' quarrel gone wrong?"

Lacey should've just taken the out there and then. But she thought of the sand filling Buck's mouth and surrounding his blue lips—evident signs he'd been held down and suffocated face-first in the sand—and blurted, "*Daisy*? No way! Buck's a big guy. Double her size. It'd take a lot of strength to overpower a man long enough to suffocate him."

"Suffocate him?" Stephen said with a gasp. "Is that how he died?"

In the doorway of her boutique, Taryn tipped her head to the side like a dog pricking its ears. Her piercing gaze became laser sharp, and Lacey noticed a small smile of delight twitch up the corners of her lips.

"Where on earth did you hear that?" Stephen finished.

Lacey paused. Damn. She'd said too much.

"Just something I heard on the grapevine," she said, aware that she was speaking with a much more rapid pace than normal but unable to stop herself. "You know, same as the gossip you heard about the sextant being stolen from the hotel room. I mean it's all speculation really, isn't it?" She giggled nervously.

"She's right about that," Taryn called out.

Stephen and Lacey turned to look at her.

"About what?" Stephen asked.

"About Daisy," Taryn qualified. "She's not the killer. She and Buck were meant to leave town today. But she's refusing to return to the states without him. Until his body's released she says she's staying put. Not exactly the behavior of a killer, is it? If I'd just killed my husband, I'd be on the first flight out of here." Her voice had grown distinctly more icy. "Especially if I'd made enemies with every single local within a five mile radius like the pair of them." She gave a nonchalant shrug. "I guess we're all going to have to put up with Miss Daisy until they figure this thing out. But we know how speedy Superintendent Turner usually is. Whoever did this won't get away with it for much longer."

Her eyes darted to Lacey again, and narrowed accusatorily. Then she retreated into her store, leaving Lacey with an uncomfortable squirming feeling in her guts.

CHAPTER NINE

L acey couldn't get inside her store fast enough. As soon as she was in, she marched in the direction of the kitchen. It had taken just a matter of weeks of living in England for a cup of tea to become the thing she reached for when in need of comfort! But she was feeling so fraught right now, so emotionally exhausted, she wasn't even sure a cuppa would be enough. Maybe a brandy would be more appropriate.

The small kitchenette came off the auction room, so she passed through the main shop floor, passing her counter, and went in through the door to the main auction room. Straight away she felt a cool breeze against her skin, and instantly glanced across the train-carriage shaped room to the glass French doors that led out into the garden. One of the panes had been smashed last month during a break in, and, not having had time to get a proper glazer over to fix the damage, was still secured by a piece of plywood fitted by the firm the police had recommended.

Lacey's first instinct was to assume the ply had somehow become detached and fallen, letting in the breeze. But no; she could see it, even from the other side of the long room. The ply was still in place. Her assumption had been wrong, and it gave way to a hitch of panic that perhaps she'd been the victim of a second break-in.

Her heartbeat began to race. She hurried toward the French doors, and was still a few meters away when she noticed that one wasn't closed, but standing an inch or two open. A shiver ran down her spine.

But the moment Lacey reached the door, she immediately realized what had happened. It wasn't another break-in at all. The keys were dangling in the lock (as they would be if someone had locked it) and the bolt was sticking out (as it would if it had been turned into the locking position). And even the dead bolt had been slid across the door, though it had not entered the catch.

Gina! Lacey thought.

Her neighbor had taken it upon herself to see to the store's garden, claiming she could cultivate a green thumb in anyone, even a New Yorker like Lacey. She must've come to the store at night to do some watering in the moonlight (according to Gina, it's the perfect time for it; plants love the combination of cool air and soft white light). But the infamously scatty woman had evidently gone through all the required steps to secure the back door again after her apart from the first and most obvious one—shutting the damn thing!

Lacey couldn't help feeling furious. The store was her pride and joy and *anything* could've happened with the place left unsecured like that! Though Wilfordshire was generally safe, it would only take one opportunistic lowlife to notice the door standing open from the footpath behind the garden to decide to strike.

Thinking of all the things she'd say to scold Gina over this, Lacey shut the door and locked it properly.

But before she had a chance to make the cup of tea she so desperately needed, she heard the front doorbell jingle. She diverted to the main store to see who had entered.

It was an innocent-looking duo—mom and young daughter—and they smiled at Lacey. She was so rattled, she had to force herself to smile in response. But in a split second, Lacey was able to put her problems aside and put her game face on.

"How are you guys today? Can I help you with anything in particular?"

She maneuvered from behind the counter to approach them. At the same moment, the door swung open again and in waltzed Taryn.

Great, Lacey thought. *That's just what I need.*

Her nemesis was obviously here to taunt her about being at a murder scene once again, only this time it would be in front of customers too!

"I need to talk to you about the footpath round the back of the gardens," Taryn said, launching into a monologue. "The hedges are overgrown and now the local kids are wedging old cans of energy drink into it."

"Can it wait?" Lacey asked her with an imploring tone. She nodded her head toward the pair standing patiently next to the shelf of frosted crystal figurines. "I have customers."

Taryn, who was always so single-minded, turned her head and flinched at the sudden presence of two people whom she'd evidently failed to even notice were there.

"When is convenient...?" she began to say, but her voice trailed off. Then her mouth dropped open as an expression of genuine disbelief appeared on her face.

Confused by what had elicited the reaction, Lacey snapped her head toward the woman and child. In an instant, she realized what Taryn had seen.

There, on the shelf behind the mother's head, nestled amongst the figurines, was the missing antique sextant.

"Did you put that there?" Lacey asked the woman.

"I'm sorry, what?" the woman said, looking perplexed.

"That!" Lacey exclaimed, stepping closer to the pair and pointing at the sextant.

The woman glanced at it fretfully. "I don't even know what it is."

"That's not what I asked. Did you bring it in with you and put it on the shelf?"

There was a slightly manic tone to her voice, Lacey was aware, but if there'd ever been a time where madness was justifiable, it was now! Because an item belonging to a murdered man was now in her possession. She being the very same person that had called in the body, and it being the very same item that Buck very well may have been murdered for! If she'd been on the jury during her trial, she'd have no doubt over her guilt at all!

"Maybe we should come back another time," the woman said suddenly, sounding disconcerted. "You seem to be busy."

She started to shoo her child toward the exit.

"But I want a ballerina!" the girl wailed.

"Wait," Lacey said to the woman. "This is important. I really need to know. Was this here when you came in?"

"Yes, of course it was," the woman said, her tone now brusque with fear. "Now leave me alone."

She shoved her daughter, and the little girl began crying. The mother didn't stop. She whisked the child away, leaving Lacey standing there reeling.

She stared at the sextant, unable to believe it.

"Well," came Taryn's haughty voice. "Isn't this a turn up for the books?"

Lacey's gaze darted back to her. "Was it you? Did you put that there?"

"Me?" Taryn exclaimed. "You literally just saw me walk in!"

"Sure, I saw you walk in through the front. But what about the back? You have easy access to my back door via the gardens. You were saying so yourself just a moment earlier."

Taryn looked unmoved by her insinuation. "Out of the two of us, you're by far the more likely person to have put it there." She pointed an accusatory finger at Lacey.

Lacey balked. "I . . . I . . ." she stammered, unable to get the words out. "I had nothing to do with it."

"Then how did it get there?" Taryn demanded, her voice warbling with malevolent glee. "What is it doing here?"

But there were no words. Lacey had no idea how the missing sextant had reappeared in her store, nor what it was doing sitting innocently on the shelves amongst the frosted crystal figurines.

"The back door was open," she said. "They must've come through there."

They. Who did she mean by *they*? Buck's murderer? The man who'd suffocated him on the beach? Or just a burglar? Whoever it was, they were a criminal, and they'd found their way into her store!

"Well, there's one thing we know for certain now," Taryn said. "Whoever stole the sextant off of Buck has a personal connection to you."

"How do we know that?" Lacey demanded.

"Because they returned the sextant to you."

Lacey paused. As much as she hated to admit it, Taryn was right. Whoever burglarized Buck's hotel room hadn't done it for personal gain. They'd done it for *her*.

"Don't touch anything," Lacey said. "There might be evidence. Footprints. Fingerprints."

But Taryn's expression had taken a sadistic turn, and Lacey noticed she was taking small steps backward toward the exit.

"Sure . . ." Taryn said, making it obvious just how much she was loving seeing Lacey flounder like this.

Lacey knew full well what Taryn was planning. Her nemesis was going to call the police on her.

"Taryn, wait . . ."

But it was too late. Taryn bolted, running out the front door, her hand already reaching into her pocket, presumably for her cell phone.

Lacey ran, too; not after Taryn, but toward her counter where the telephone was.

She grabbed the received and jabbed the hash key followed by the number 4. After everything that had happened with Iris Archer's murder, she'd programmed the local Wilfordshire police into her speed dial settings. At the time, she'd lamented the fact they were her fourth most dialed number (after Naomi, Tom and her mother) but now she was glad for it. The quicker she spoke to Superintendent Turner, the quicker she'd be able to mitigate against Taryn's accusations.

Through the speaker, she heard the call begin ringing. Then the call connected and Lacey heard the sound of the far-too-familiar greeting.

"Good morning, Wilfordshire police, how can I help you?"

"I need to speak with Superintendent Turner," Lacey said.

"He's not in the office yet. Can I take a message? What's it about?"

"Can you transfer me to his cell?"

The woman on the other end paused. "No, I'm sorry that isn't possible."

"I know it is," Lacey said, recalling the numerous times she'd seen him take work calls on his personal cell with her very own eyes. She knew she was starting to sound desperate now. "Please. I know Karl personally. He'll want to take my call."

"Can you give me your name please?"

"Lacey Doyle."

The woman repeated her name aloud, but Lacey was still speaking, and her desperate pleas drowned out her words.

"Please, it's important, I need to—"

"—Lacey?" The voice of Superintendent Turner came through the speaker. Lacey paused. "Wait. What? You're there?"

"I just walked into the station and overheard your name. What's going on?"

Lacey tightened her grip on the phone, wondering if she was about to make a terrible mistake, but knowing full well that she had no other option.

She swallowed, hard.

"I have some very important information related to the murder of Buckland Stringer."

CHAPTER TEN

Superintendent Turner's shadow stretched over Lacey. She'd slumped into one of the fashionable armchairs in the Nordic corner of her store while she'd been waiting for the detectives to arrive, and he was now standing directly in front of a stylish bronze 1970s Art Deco overreach floor lamp. Its beams were casting a bright halo of light all around him and turning him into a big, black looming silhouette.

"Please. Sit down," Lacey repeated, squinting against the glare.

The detective took a cursory glance at the bright orange velour couch, then his gaze flicked back to meet hers. He flipped open his notebook.

"Tell me again what happened," he began. "And by 'what happened,' I mean what you *know* to have happened, not what you guess could have happened, or assume might have happened, or figured was probably most likely to have happened."

Lacey felt herself cringe internally; not because of the tone the detective was taking with her, of a displeased schoolmaster, but because he was so on the nose in his assessment of her. She *did* have a habit of assuming and supposing and guessing and figuring. It was half the reason she always landed herself in hot water.

Just then, DCI Beth Lewis turned to look over her shoulder from where she was standing beside the shelves. She'd been gazing intently at the sextant this whole time, her hands deep in the pockets of her camel-colored trench coat. As she removed her hands from her pockets, taking her notebook out of one and a pen out of the other, the fabric made a pleasing swishing noise.

"So you noticed the sextant was there when you opened up the store this morning," she said, with a ponderous tone and a slightly furrowed brow. "Is that correct?"

Lacey looked from one detective to the next. The pair of them looked like ghoulish apparitions.

"Yes," she said. Then she backtracked. "No, not quite. I mean, not right away."

She rubbed the spot between her eyebrows. She'd already been through everything with Superintendent Turner. Repeating it all over again was frustrating, especially because Lacey knew it was a police tactic to try to find inconsistencies in her statements. She'd have to be very careful about how she relayed the story for a second time.

"I came in through the front of the store," she said with precision, visualizing the moment again. "I headed straight through this room into the auction room and toward the kitchenette to make a cup of tea. I felt a breeze as I entered and noticed the back door was open. My friend Gina is doing up the garden. She likes to water under moonlight. She must've left it open last night. She's quite scatty. She always forgets to lock her gate and then her sheep come and graze on my lawn."

She trailed off. DCI Lewis's eyebrows were slowly rising, and Lacey knew that one of the surest signs of a liar was someone who gave way too much useless information. The extra detail about Gina might be easily construed that way, but it *was* the truth, and it did explain why the door had been left open. Lacey decided it was relevant information, albeit convoluted, so she continued with her explanation.

"Before I had a chance to do anything about the back door, the bell in here rang." She pointed at it—as if it was evidence that proved she wasn't a blathering madwoman—but neither of the detectives looked, and she continued to squirm under their scrutiny. "So I came back in to see to my customer, a woman and her daughter. My neighbor Taryn, from the boutique next door, she came in to talk about the footpath behind our gardens, and then we both sort of spotted the sextant at the same time. The customer swore she didn't bring it in with her, but I didn't see her enter so there's a chance she might have."

She noticed Superintendent Turner's frown deepen, and realized she'd slipped in a *might*.

"Sorry," she said, her voice trailing away. "That's just an assumption."

"Was that recording?" DCI Lewis asked, pointing her pen at the security camera in the corner of the store. "We could check to see if the woman brought it in with her."

Lacey shook her head. "I hadn't even booted up the system yet."

Superintendent Turner rolled his eyes. "I'll never understand store owners scrimping on their security systems. You know Taryn next door has a top of the line one, state of the art. HD quality. I bet you couldn't find a better system in Downing Street. It's been a godsend for establishing alibis."

Lacey folded her arms. "Taryn's business is a little more established than mine, Karl."

She used his Christian name, as she often did when he was annoying her and she felt like he'd lost his privilege of respect. Then she paused. Something Superintendent Turner had said had flagged in her mind. "What do you mean it's been a godsend for establishing alibis? Alibis for who? *Taryn?*"

She couldn't quite believe she was uttering that aloud. Her neighbor was a meanie, it was true, but a murderer? Surely not.

DCI Lewis turned her head sharply to her partner and glared at him, as if she could communicate her disapproval of him accidentally leaking classified information to a civilian telepathically. Maybe she could. Superintendent Turner coughed into his fist awkwardly.

"Does Gina have keys to the store then?" DCI Lewis asked, flipping open her notebook and clicking the top of her pen.

"Yes," Lacey confirmed.

"Does anyone else?"

"My landlord, Stephen," Lacey said. She stopped, recalling how she'd bumped into him in the streets just moments before discovering the sextant in her store. Could *he* have put it there? He had access, after all. But Stephen? Her unassuming landlord?

The two detectives were now glaring down at her with the most suspicious looks, and Lacey realized she'd trailed off and was staring into the distance as her paranoid brain found suspicion in everyone.

"Lacey?" Superintendent Turner asked. "Did you think of something relevant?"

Lacey shook her head. "No. It's nothing."

The last thing she wanted to do was point the finger at anyone, or draw the detectives suspicions toward them.

"Is there anyone else you can think of who might be able to access your store?" DCI Lewis asked, steering the conversation back on track.

"No," Lacey said. "Actually, the tenants who leased the store before me might. They left in a hurry, without giving notice. Didn't pay their bills, left a valuable, antique lamp shade behind, so I can imagine them going off with the keys as well. Oh, except they're both deceased so I guess it's not likely to be them."

Superintendent Turner ground his teeth.

"Sorry," Lacey muttered, realizing she'd done it again.

DCI Lewis sank into the gaudy orange couch. "Say someone did come in through your back door," she began.

Superintendent Turner let out a frustrated sigh and paced away, taking his turn to peer at the sextant.

The female detective rolled her eyes in a *don't mind him* kind of way. "What do you think would be their reason for returning the sextant?"

Lacey shifted uncomfortably. She knew it was unwise to ruminate on this with the police—how many criminals had been caught out by the old, "if you *had* done it, what would you have done?" method, after all?—but it was too tempting for Lacey to resist.

"To frame me," she blurted.

Beth Lewis nodded as if she'd thought the same thing. "Why do you think someone would want to frame you? Have you made any enemies?"

Lacey just about managed to hold her tongue and not blurt out Taryn's name. Instead, she calmly replied, "I don't think that's why. It's not someone trying to frame me because I'm their enemy, they're framing me because I'm the obvious suspect. I found the body. I sold the sextant. I have more connections to Buck than anyone else in Wilfordshire, and the clearest motive. If there's anyone to set up, it would be me."

DCI Lewis nodded slowly. Lacey tried to read her eyes but it was impossible to tell what she was thinking. At least there was a chance with DCI Lewis that she'd consider Lacey's differing opinion. Superintendent Turner was certainly incapable of it.

Just then the front door swung violently open, making the bell above it clang rather than tinkle, and a flash of bright pink swirled into the store.

Lacey sat straight up, surprised to see Daisy was staggering in on her pink high heels. Her eyes were wet with tears. Mascara ran down her cheeks.

"There you are!" she bellowed, pointing a shaking finger at Superintendent Turner. She was filled with rage. "I shouldn't have to ask the local barmaid if she knows where I can find the detectives on the case of my husband's murder!" Her voice grew shriller with each word.

Lacey felt the need to avert her eyes. Daisy's grief was indisputable, but it looked far closer to fury than sadness, and the whole thing left Lacey feeling uncomfortable.

"So?" Daisy demanded of Karl. "What have you got to say for yourself?"

From the back room, Lacey heard the sound of Chester scrabbling at the door. She'd shut him in so as to avoid any more of Superintendent Turner's snide comments regarding him, and the commotion must have roused him. He probably thought she was in danger, with all that shrieking going on.

"Perhaps you should come to the station for us to talk about it," Superintendent Turner said.

He attempted to steer Daisy toward the door with an outstretched arm, but the woman was not about to comply. She sidestepped him, contorting her body as she moved out of his reach. And that was when it happened.

Daisy saw the sextant.

Her expression turned to horror, like she'd just seen someone coming back from the dead.

"What is that doing here!" she screeched. "That's mine! That's the item that was stolen! That's the reason Buck was killed!"

She totally lost it then. She fell to her knees and dissolved into a puddle of tears.

Lacey could bear it no longer. Neither of the detectives was doing anything to comfort the grieving woman. Leaving her to cry alone in a heap on the floor like that just didn't feel right to Lacey. She stood from the swanky Nordic armchair and paced over to Daisy.

"Let me help you up," she said.

But the second she laid a hand on the woman's shoulder, Daisy turned her head sharply up to Lacey and glared at her.

"Don't you touch me! You . . . you . . . murderer!"

She screamed so loudly the sound carried into the street, and a bunch of people walking by turned to look. A small huddle started to form at the window. DCI Lewis strode over, waving her arms as if to shoo them away. At the sight of a police officer, the curious crowd scurried away.

"Why aren't you arresting her?" Daisy wailed. "Don't you see? She killed my Bucky. She's a crook. He paid her fair and square for the sextant and she killed him to get it back!"

Just then, the back door that led into the auction room opened and in flew Chester. He'd managed to leap up and pull down the handle!

He tore like a furry bullet across the shop floor toward Daisy.

Time seemed to slow down for Lacey. She could see every moment with crystal clear precision.

"CHESTER!" Lacey bellowed, suddenly afraid he might bite the woman, just as he had done with Nigel when he'd broken in.

There was hesitation in Chester's movements. He knew well enough he was supposed to obey Lacey when she used her stern voice, but he'd pushed the boundary of her tolerance once before in order to get to the island and had gotten away with it, then, so why not try again. Lacey worried that he might do the same again, only with far worse consequences. Biting a grieving widow, even if she'd accused Lacey of murder, was not okay! And doing it in front of a police officer, well, he'd end up on his way to the vet to be put down!

"Chester," she said again, deeper, even more sternly.

Finally, the dog skidded to a halt.

Everyone stared at him, stunned into silence.

Daisy scrabbled to her feet. DCI Lewis sprang into action, clasping her elbow to help her up. "Come on, let's go back to the station and talk you through everything we've been doing with the investigation so far."

The two women left—one every inch the dignified model of composure, the other a gibbering wreck—and Lacey was left alone with Superintendent Turner.

"Your dog," he said, looking at Chester. "Is he trained properly?"

"Yes," Lacey said, quickly. "He follows my commands. Apart from that one time on the island but I guess he must've ... smelled the body." Her voice trailed sadly away, as she recalled once more the horrifying sight of the deceased Buck.

"Did he used to be a police dog?" Superintendent Turner asked.

It was the first time he'd shown an actual interest in him, rather than making jokes about him.

"I don't know," Lacey said. "He sort of came with the store. I adopted him because the old tenants are deceased." She paused. "Why do you ask?"

"The way he acted just then. It looked exactly like our canine units when they're about to take down a suspect."

Lacey regarded the detective. He was usually quite good at hiding his true emotions, and hiding the inner most workings of his mind, but this time it was obvious. He suspected Daisy.

"It couldn't have been her," Lacey said. "It just couldn't. She was half Buck's size. There's no way she'd be able to overpower him."

"No. Definitely not. But maybe there was an opportunity and she took it. I mean, the man suffocated on sand. He wasn't strangled. There was distance between him and the murderer. It was cold. They didn't want to get their hands dirty. Didn't want to chip a nail. If he fell—a heart problem, possibly, a big man like him was bound to have one—and rather than help him up, she pushed her stiletto into his back. When he's already vulnerable, unable to fight back, in the middle of a medical emergency, she made certain he wouldn't wake back up."

Lacey realized he was now musing aloud, as if he'd entirely forgotten she was there. She stayed silent, curious to hear his theory play out.

"But why? Was there abuse? Was she set to inherit money? It wouldn't be the first time a pretty young woman married an older man for his money..." Suddenly, his head snapped up and he stared at Lacey as if seeing her for the first time. It almost looked like he'd come out of a trance and was shocked to discover he wasn't in the station theorizing with DCI Lewis, but standing in an antiques furniture store talking to a woman he seemed to despise.

"Don't repeat what I just said to anyone," he said, abruptly.

"Of course I won't," Lacey said. She mimed zipping her lips. "Do you really think it might've been Daisy? But what about the sextant? Why would she claim it had been stolen, only to then return it?"

"To frame you," he said, simply. "Just like you said. You're the easiest person to blame."

"Huh," Lacey said.

For what felt like the first time ever, she and Superintendent Turner saw eye to eye on something.

The man glanced over his shoulder at the waiting police cruiser, DCI Lewis watching him impatiently from the front, Daisy hunched over in the back, her shoulders shaking from evident tears.

He looked back at Lacey. "Don't leave town, okay?"

"I don't plan on it," Lacey replied.

And with that, he left.

CHAPTER ELEVEN

Lacey already knew what would happen next. Gossip. She braced herself. It would take all of ten minutes for each store owner on the high street to pass on the news to the next along, and the next after that, like a game of Telephone. It wouldn't take long before everyone in town knew that the sextant had been discovered in Lacey's store, propelling her right into the center of a murderer investigation. *A second* murder investigation, no less.

Lacey knew how it worked. The fact she had nothing to do with the slaying of Iris—something the police themselves had declared—would count for nothing. People would still think it was too remarkable a concurrence of events to be mere coincidence. She was going to become a suspect again, if not in the police, then in the minds of everyone in Wilfordshire. And she didn't know if she had the strength to go through all that for a second time.

It took less than an hour for people to stop coming into her store. Her usual flow of customers dwindled to a trickle, before drying up entirely. This was another outcome that Lacey had anticipated. Last time, she'd almost lost her business over the lack of trade. She'd been exceptionally lucky to recover, and that was in large part due to Nigel choosing her to auction Iris's entire estate. Without the commission she'd earned, she'd have gone bankrupt. But that was a one off. Now she relied on the income from sales to stay afloat and she was not going to be getting anything resembling a steady trade as long as Buck's murder was hanging over her head.

She had no choice. She would have to find out what happened and clear her name.

Good thing I've got so much free time now, she thought dryly.

There was no point standing around hoping someone would come in, so she closed up shop and headed across the street to Tom's to fill him in on everything that had transpired with the cops, and get some much needed TLC.

As she entered the patisserie, she discovered he was swamped with customers. They all seemed to sidestep as she entered, and she noticed people whispering behind their hands. She kept her chin up high and edged her way to the counter.

"Tom," she said, trying to get his attention. He seemed extremely focused on boxing up a slice of gooey chocolate cream cake.

He looked up, the business in his eyes evident. "Lacey? What are you doing here? Is everything okay?"

"Not really," she said.

"What's wrong?" he asked.

"It's the sextant," Lacey said, having to project her voice over the thrum of noise in the patisserie." It turned up at my store."

"The what?" Tom asked, straining as if he'd been unable to hear her over the noisy customers.

"The antique! Someone put it in my store. Gina left the door unlocked." She squeezed her hand into a fist, and muttered to herself, "I am going to kill her."

A woman standing beside Lacey looked suddenly perturbed. She took a big step back.

"I don't mean literally," Lacey began. "It's just a figure of speech."

But her explanation fell on deaf ears. The woman was looking away and ignoring her.

There'll be more of this to come, Lacey thought. *This is just the beginning.*

She turned back to Tom. A girl was blocking her view of him. But then she moved away, a prettily decorated pink cupcake in her hands.

Lacey beelined for her usual stool at the counter and slunk onto it before any other customers came in and interrupted them.

"What am I going to do?" she asked Tom. "Superintendent Turner let slip that Daisy's their prime suspect, but that doesn't mean I'm not one as well." She let her head drop into her hands. "I can't believe this is happening to me," she lamented. "Again. It was bad enough last time. I don't know if I have the energy to go through it all over again."

She got no response from Tom and raised her head up from her hands. He'd disappeared into the kitchen while she was talking. Lacey felt a stab of disappointment in her chest.

A moment later, he reemerged with a huge tub filled with chocolate marzipan.

"Sorry, Lacey. Paul was meant to help me today but he called in sick. Now I have fifteen marzipan ferrets to make for a wedding this afternoon. Apparently, the bride and groom are avid ferret breeders. I wouldn't want rodents on my wedding cake, no matter how much I loved them, but there you go. Each to their own."

Lacey stood motionless, unable to do anything but blink at him. "Tom. I'm being scapegoated for a murder. And you're worrying about ferrets?"

He frowned. "This is my job."

"This is my *life!*"

"I know, I didn't mean that. I'm not trying to compete with you. I'm just saying it's important. I can't just let the ball drop because of some silly rumors. We've been through this before. It will blow over once the police solve everything."

"Once the police solve everything? I'm sorry, but don't you remember how much effort we had to go through last time? How much of the investigation we had to do ourselves? The police are blinkered when it comes to these matters. They've already proven as much. I've been set up and if I don't clear my name, then they'll just take the easy route and blame me."

As she spoke, Tom had begun working on the ferrets. She realized his attention had cut out somewhere before the end of her monologue.

She stood. "I'll go."

"No. Stay with me. You hate it when the town's whispering about you, so you may as well stay in here and not listen."

But Lacey was too irritated. She had to leave. "I'll speak to you later. Good luck with the ferrets."

She swirled out of the patisserie, feeling completely alone. But more than that, she felt determined. She was going to have to work out what happened and clear her name. She'd done it before, she could do it again.

She crossed the cobblestone streets and went back inside her customerless store. She sat down at the counter and retrieved her notebook from the drawer beneath the old bronze register, and turned to a blank page. She drew a Venn diagram—a circle on one half of the page, and another on the other half, the two shapes overlapping in the middle. Above the left circle, she wrote, "MO for murder," and above the right circle she wrote, "MO for theft." Then she began to fill the circles with everyone and anyone she could think of who might fit into either of the circles, or, more importantly, the overlapping section in the middle.

Daisy went straight into the "MO for murder" circle. She was swiftly followed by Ed, Brenda's boyfriend who'd squared up to him in the pub. Of all the suspects he had a clear and obvious motive *but* he had literally no connection to the sextant.

Over on the "MO for theft" side, she wrote *Stephen (has keys)*, even though she couldn't think of any actual possible reason he'd be involved. Then she added another name: *mysterious Spanish man.*

She sat back and stared at the right hand circle. The handsome man who'd come to her auction—no, *flown* specifically to her auction—had wanted the sextant very badly, but was beaten by Buck. Could he have had something to do with its theft? But then why return it to her? Why not just steal it and fly back to Spain while everyone was distracted with the murder?

She turned to a fresh, blank paper, and began scrawling different scenarios that might explain the foreigner's behavior, if there was a chance he'd been involved.

Killed Buck because he beat him in the auction? Killed Buck to cause distraction in order to steal the sextant? Returned the sextant to my store because . . .

She stopped writing. It made no sense. The Spanish man might have had an MO to steal the sextant, but not to return it to her store. Then she clicked her fingers, as a memory from the auction came to her mind's eye; the Spanish man checking his watch, leaving early, his comment that he had a plane to catch, the mix-up over the time zone difference which led to his being in a rush in the first place.

"He wasn't even in the country," Lacey said, thinking aloud.

She screwed up the second page and threw it in her wastepaper basket, scoring a perfect 3-pointer, then turned back to the Venn diagram and drew a neat line through the words *mysterious Spanish man.* Instead, she added his name to the left-hand column, because there was still a possibility he killed Buck because the man had beaten him in the auction.

But then she crossed him out again. The Spanish man was flying out of England straight after the auction! He'd been anxious about missing his flight home, and kept looking at his watch. There would've been no time at all for him to kill Buck. Lacey let out a breath of relief to know there was at least one person she could rule off the list. That just left her with every woman and shop owner in Wilfordshire to work through!

"What a mess," Lacey said, sighing.

Chester raised his head from his paws and let out his own whistling sigh, as if mirroring her. She couldn't help but feel thankful for her furry companion. At least Chester was always on her side.

She looked back down at her circles. They'd become kind of messy. Her attention fell to Daisy. Lacey was still convinced that a woman could not have killed Buck, especially one as small as Daisy. She was about to put a line through *harassed women* when she recalled what Superintendent Turner had accidentally revealed to her while he'd been musing aloud. If Buck had been in the middle of a medical emergency, perhaps someone smaller than him could have been able to overpower him?

She turned to a new blank page, and repeated the same process she had with the mystery Spanish man with Daisy.

Daisy killed Buck because of a lovers' quarrel. She returned the sextant to my store to throw the investigation, and make it look like the two events were connected. She came in and accused me of murder in front of the police. Was she trying to control the narrative? She'd have to be an amazing actress to pull off that grief routine. Although . . . she did seem more angry than grief-stricken.

She sat back, pondering. Daisy did seem like a viable suspect after all. And Lacey had been able to find an MO for the sextant as well. She turned back to her circles, and moved Daisy into the central overlapping section.

"Am I giving her too much credit, Chester?" she asked the dog. "I mean, she didn't seem smart enough to pull off something elaborate like that."

Chester whined. Lacey decided to leave Daisy in the central position for now. She was the only name that could possibly overlap. And that was the most likely person to be the murderer, wasn't it? Someone who killed Buck and planted the sextant to frame her.

"Unless . . ." Lacey said, tapping her pen on the paper.

What if she'd been going about this the wrong way, by assuming the two events were even related? She remembered Superintendent Turner's warning, about making assumptions and guesses. There was nothing concrete that *proved* the two events were connected, and though Occam's razor would suggest they were, it wouldn't hurt to consider the possibility they weren't. Besides, she'd thought Iris's murderer had burgled her store, and that had turned out to be incorrect. Maybe the sextant and the murder were unconnected?

"Let's say, for argument's sake," Lacey said aloud, "that the sextant wasn't stolen from Buck at all. Rather he dropped it on the floor in the hotel lobby, and Roger from the English Antiques Society found it and returned it to me via my open back door." It was far-fetched, but she was only spit-balling. "Who would that open up the suspect pool to include? I'm sure Brenda's wasn't the only butt Buck smacked, so there'd be some other women on the list."

She wondered where Buck and Daisy had been staying while in Wilfordshire. Then she remembered Tom cleaning Buck's spat out chocolate on the floor of his patisserie and remembered what he'd told her: Carol's B'n'B. It made sense as well. The frontage was cotton-candy pink. It would have proven too much of a lure for Daisy to pass up.

Lacey added, '*staff at Carol's B'n'B?*' onto her list, certain more than a few of them had had unpleasant encounters with Buck, similar to Brenda. She quickly added, '*other harassed women?*'

"May as well open up my suspect list to fifty percent of the population," Lacey said wryly. "Who else?"

She chewed her pen, ponderously. Then she wrote '*every disgruntled shop owner in Wilfordshire?*'

She let out a frustrated sigh and threw the pen down.

Every single store owner on the high street had a reason to hate Buck. He and Daisy made enemies out of everyone! Everyone had a motive.

"Heck, even Tom could be on the list," Lacey said.

Then she paused. Tom fit into the first circle like everyone else, but he was actually connected to both the murder *and* the sextant. He had reason to hate Buck, and reason to return the antique to her store. That meant he fitted in the middle section, along with Daisy.

Lacey added his name and stared at it.

In her heart, she knew it couldn't be him. But he would certainly be on Superintendent Turner and DCI Lewis's list of suspects along with her. Possibly even higher than her, since he was more of a physical match for Buck.

"He shouldn't have been so flippant earlier," she said, exhaling. "Because Tom might very well become embroiled in all this as well."

There was no time to waste. If Lacey wanted to make any headway, she'd have to track Buck and Daisy's whole experience in the town and find out who they upset on the way. And she knew just the place to start: Carol's cotton-candy-pink B'n'B.

"Come on, Chester," Lacey said to her loyal pooch. "It's sleuthing time."

CHAPTER TWELVE

Lacey hadn't set foot inside the B'n'B since her very first day in Wilfordshire, when she'd assumed she'd easily be able to find a room. It felt strange being inside again. As she glanced around at the lurid pink walls and plastic flamingo decorations, she couldn't help but wonder about how her life would have turned out completely differently if there had been a spare room for her here. She'd never have bumped into Ivan who rented her Crag Cottage, which meant she would never have met Gina.

Gina who showed me the island that I later discovered a dead body on, she thought, getting caught up in one of those butterfly effect moments.

She shook her head. You could drive yourself crazy with thoughts like those!

"Can I help you?" a female voice said, seemingly from nowhere.

Lacey startled. She hadn't noticed the person sitting at the reception desk, since they were obscured behind a fan of leaves from an overgrown fern plant that took up half the desk.

Lacey tipped her head to the side to look around the fern leaves, and a young woman appeared in her line of sight. She was very pretty, dark haired and olive skinned, with a huge red flower in her hair. In the chintzy surroundings, Lacey was half expecting her to leap up and start flamenco dancing, but instead she just sat there, staring at her expectantly. Lacey read the name on the bronze lettered broach attached to her fussy, frilly, red silk uniform: Carla.

"Hi, Carla," Lacey began, taking a step forward. "I was wondering if I could ask you some questions."

Chester, ever her shadow, followed her step, and Carla suddenly leaped up from her seat.

"You can't bring your dog in here," she began. But then recognition flashed in her eyes. "Hey, you're the dog from the antiques shop, aren't you? What are you doing in here? Are you being a good boy?"

Her tone for Chester was significantly more polite than it had been when she'd been addressing Lacey. And since she appeared to be directing the conversation toward the dog, Lacey was put in that awkward position of having to communicate through him.

"Yes, this is Chester," she said. "My antique stores protector."

"Is that right?" Carla said, still speaking directly to Chester, using the same baby voice as before. "Are you a special guard doggy? Are you? Do you keep the antiques store safe?"

Lacey suddenly hit on an idea. Chester could be her in!

"He does," she said, cringing a little at the sound of her own voice adopting Carla's baby-speak voice. "He's a very special guard doggy. He's looking for the person who killed Buck, aren't you, Chester? You want to catch the killer so everyone in Wilfordshire can be safe again."

At the mention of Buck's name, Carla's face darted back up to meet Lacey's. She looked suddenly very animated. Lacey pegged her for a gossiper. You could always tell by the way their eyes bulged at the smallest whiff of drama.

"Buck? The guy who got murdered? You know he was staying here, right? Him and his wife. The police are putting her up in special accommodations at the moment but she hasn't packed any of their stuff up yet, and we're not allowed to touch their room in case there's evidence."

Just as Lacey suspected, Carla's tongue had become suddenly loose. She didn't want to judge the girl; she was young, after all, and this was probably the most exciting thing that had happened to her, living in a small and uneventful British seaside town, but her excitement came across as a little crass to Lacey.

"What was he like?" Lacey asked. "Was he a good guest?"

"No, he was a nightmare," the girl said dramatically, gesturing with her hands as she spoke. "He demanded we upgrade him to the honeymoon suite for free because we'd advertised sea views and his room didn't have one. Then he pretended he was allergic to nuts and said he'd sue if we didn't let him have free dinners. Then he claimed he saw a rat in his room and said he'd call the health inspectors if he didn't get a discount. I mean, poor Carol. He was already costing her more than she was earning, and now he's dead, she'll probably never see a penny."

"She didn't take his card details on check-in?" Lacey asked, thinking of the various hotels she'd stayed in during business trips, back when she worked for Saskia. It was standard practice to take card details in case the guest left without paying for their extras—using the minibar, the hot tub, or, as was probably likely in Buck's case, the adult channels. Lacey shuddered at the thought.

"He flat out refused," Carla told her. "Went on some huge rant about how his money was as good as the next person's. He even waved this stack of notes under her nose until she backed down!"

Lacey recalled the moment he'd done the exact same thing to her, waving his money around, refusing to put his 10% down payment for the sextant on card, demanding he be allowed to circumvent the usual protocols and get special treatment. Clearly, it was a trick he'd used all around town.

"This is a bit of a sensitive question," Lacey said, lowering her voice now. "But did any of the staff complain about him being suggestive, or making advances? I'm sorry to ask, it's just that other people said he was a bit handsy with them and I'm wondering...I mean *Chester* is wondering...if that might have been related to the killer's motive."

Carla shook her head of glossy dark hair. "Luckily, I was never alone with him. But some of the chambermaids complained to Carol. I'm not sure if anything happened in the end, but Stanislav, the chef here, demanded in a staff meeting that Carol call the police, because if she didn't, he'd poison Buck's breakfast!"

She laughed like it was obviously a joke, but Lacey didn't see the funny side. It was never okay to threaten harm to another person any way, but for that person to later turn up dead, well, then it seemed like karma trying to teach an important lesson. Especially since his comment was going to earn Stanislav a spot on her suspects chart.

"So they ate breakfast here?" Lacey continued, trying to get as much information out of Carla before she twigged that was spilling confidential information. "What about evening meals?"

"Not usually," Carla replied. "They would usually be out at night and come home in the early hours of the morning. Some of the other guests complained about how noisy they were when they came in."

"Do you know where they ate?" Lacey asked.

For the first time since her questioning had begun, Carla looked at Lacey suspiciously. "Why do you want to know that?" she asked.

"Just curious," Lacey replied. "It's a mystery, and as far as we know, there's a murderer on the loose in Wilfordshire."

"Sure..." Carla said, but her drawn out tone was filled with skepticism.

Just then, Lacey noticed the stack of glossy pamphlets on the reception desk. One was a map of Wilfordshire produced by the National Trust, detailing historical places of significance and countryside walks. One was a program of events produced by the local theatre. The third listed local eateries. Anytime she was in a new area, she'd pick up one of these pamphlets to know where to eat. Perhaps Buck and Daisy did the same?

Lacey took one, under the watchful glare of Carla.

"For the coupons," she muttered in an excuse. "Thanks for your time."

She left, Chester following along with her.

So her hunch had been right about Buck pestering the staff.

She opened the pamphlet. Gianni's Pizzeria was the first ad her eyes fell to. Lacey had only been to the quaint, family-run eatery once on a date with Tom, but it was as good a place to start as any.

She went along the high street to the Italian restaurant. It was a small place, with a genuine clay pizza oven and shelves filled with very expensive pasta products. It was super cozy inside.

Gianni's son was on duty today, a nice-looking guy in his mid-thirties whom Lacey only knew by sight and not name.

"Can I help?" he asked.

Lacey felt like she'd made herself seem a bit suspicious in Carol's, so she decided to take a more subtle approach this time. Since Gianni's sold produce, this was the perfect place for her to also source the fresh ingredients she'd need to make homemade pizza for Tom, so her incognito plan fell quickly into place.

"I wondered if you could help me with a little challenge I've been given," she said. "I have to make a pizza from scratch. Dough and all. Could you show me what to buy? Give me some tips?"

"Of course," the man said, more than happy to help.

He came over to the shelves and stood beside her, looking up at the array of packets and jars. He took down a fancy looking bag of pizza dough flour blend with an eye-wateringly high price tag that Lacey chose to avert her eyes from.

"Horrible business about that dead man," Lacey said, jumping in before the man had a chance to start explaining to her about the flour.

"Yes. Terrible," he replied.

"Every store along the high street is freaked," Lacey said. "Did you ever serve him?"

"Oh yes. Him and his wife. She had expensive taste in wine. And he seemed incapable of telling her no."

Lacey raised an eyebrow, her curiosity piqued. She'd seen Daisy cajoling Buck into parting with his money with her own eyes at the auction, but had assumed that was a one-off because she wanted the sextant so badly. But by the sounds of things, that behavior was more of a habit. "Sounds like there's a story there," Lacey said.

The server nodded and grabbed a drinks menu from the counter. "Buck asked if they could have a wine that went well with seafood, and she folded her arms and pouted and demanded the expensive one." He passed the menu to Lacey, pointing at the top right hand page where the most expensive bottles were listed. His finger had landed on a Montepulciano d'Abruzzo. "She asked for 'mont-pul-key-ano.' She mispronounced the word, and so I asked her again what she meant, and she huffed and said, 'I want the most expensive one.' She did not know anything about the grape or region per se, only that it was the most expensive one on the menu. And Buck relented and ordered it."

His story was remarkably similar to Lacey's own experience of the couple, with Daisy goading Buck on to buy the sextant.

"Did he pay for the meal?" she asked, recalling the stories of how Buck would send meals back to the kitchen after having eaten at least half of them. "Some other business owners on the high street have said he didn't."

The man put a hand up to his mouth in sudden realization. "Oh. You're right. He'd left his card in his hotel room and since my father is such a kind Italian man he said that it was alright if he paid next time he came in. But I don't think he did, come to think of it. Oh no. We'll be out of pocket now."

"Darn," Lace said.

She bought the ingredients for the pizza and left.

She tried the next eatery along from Gianni's, a tapas bar, and got a similar story. Buck had bought a ton of expensive plates on the urging of Daisy, before claiming he'd left his card in his hotel room and promising payment once he'd retrieved it, then failing to return. It seemed the couple had played the same trick almost every night they'd been in Wilfordshire.

It was certainly a very interesting piece of the puzzle that helped build up a bigger picture. But it also meant Lacey's suspect pool was becoming ever wider with every store she entered. Aside from Gianni, there wasn't a single business proprietor on the high street who'd not been offended by Buck and Daisy during their short stay. And it seemed like most of them only tolerated their BS because of the amount of money they thought they were spending.

By the time Lacey made it to the end of the high street—Chester beside her the whole way—a spring shower had started, and she was quickly coated in a thin layer of drizzle, something her naturally curly hair was particularly opposed to. Luckily, there was only one more place left on the high street for Lacey to go to, and it was also the place she least wanted to. The Coach House Inn. The pub was such a hotbed for gossip, Lacey would much prefer to turn around and march the other way. But Brenda's boyfriend Ed was one of her top suspects, and there'd be people inside who witnessed the altercation between him and Buck. She was bound to learn something relevant if she plucked up the courage to go inside. She'd most certainly get stared at, but clearing her name depended on it, and so she headed toward the stained glass doors.

But before she reached the doors, someone pulled them open from inside the pub. Out they came, striding quickly, head bowed against the drizzle, almost bumping right into her.

"*Lo siento,*" he said, raising his gaze to meet Lacey's.

She gasped. She was staring into cocoa-colored eyes of the mysterious Spanish man.

Chapter Thirteen

Lacey was completely lost for words. All she could do was stare at the man. Seeing him in Wilfordshire when she'd expected to never see him again had taken her completely by surprise.

"It is you," the man said, breaking the silence. "Do you remember me? Xavier, from the auction."

Finally, Lacey came back to her senses.

"What are you doing back in Wilfordshire?" she managed to stammer.

"I never left," he replied. "I missed my flight home."

"You've been in Wilfordshire since the auction?" Lacey asked, shocked. "Then that means you've been here the whole time."

Her voice died in her throat. By *the whole time*, Lacey really meant *the whole time since Buck's murder*, and a sense of disquiet overcame her as she visualized her Venn diagram. She'd only crossed the mysterious Spanish man off her list of suspects because she thought he'd left for the airport immediately following the sale of the sextant, and well before Buck was discovered dead. But if he'd been in town the whole time, then he was back on the list. He'd put himself right back in the frame as Buck's possible killer.

"By the whole time, you mean during this whole police business, do you not?" Xavier said, glancing furtively behind him, over one shoulder then the next. "I know what you are thinking. You are thinking *I* had something to do with the American man's death, just like everyone else."

Lacey could see the look of anguish in his chocolate brown eyes. She wanted desperately to believe that the emotion in them was genuine, but she was no fool. She couldn't trust him.

"You took me by surprise, that's all," she told him, trying to keep her tone steady so as not to betray her discomfort. "I haven't seen you around and it's a pretty small town, I would've expected to bump into you at some point. Where are you staying?"

He jabbed a thumb over his shoulder toward the Coach House Inn standing behind him.

"There?" Lacey asked, getting her second shock of the evening that no one had gossiped about him being there.

"I have been holed up," Xavier continued hurriedly, his voice hushed. "I knew straight away me still being here would look highly suspicious, considering what happened. But I can assure you I had nothing to do with that man's death."

His use of distancing language wasn't lost on Lacey. First, he'd referred to Buck as the American man, then an even more vague version: that man. He'd referred to the murder as police business, a death, and something that had happened. From a linguistical analysis perspective, it didn't look good for Xavier. But at the same time, there was a sense of urgency in his tone, and a look of desperation in his eyes. All his non-verbal communication was screaming that he was an innocent man caught up in something far beyond him. Maybe his distancing word choices were due to the language difference and the fact that English wasn't his mother tongue? That could explain the incongruency. But it couldn't explain the fact that he was here, in Wilfordshire, when flights from London to Spain were a dime a dozen.

Lacey decided to stay firmly on the fence about Xavier, and keep her mind as open as possible. She had a lot more digging to do.

"I don't mean to sound rude," Lacey said, "but why *are* you still here? If you missed your first flight, wasn't there a later one you could book onto?"

Xavier ran his hands through his dark hair, looking suddenly agitated. "Everything was fully booked. The British, they love a cheap holiday in the Spanish sunshine. There was space on a flight early the next morning, but it was already too late by then. The police intercepted me at the train station, while I was sitting on my train waiting for it to depart for Heathrow. It was so humiliating! I must have looked like a criminal to everyone in that carriage. It was six in the morning! The man had only been dead a matter of hours, yet they had already managed to track my movements and follow me all the way to Exeter city. To move that fast, they must have immediately decided I was a suspect. They told me they were only questioning me as an important witness, but I can read between the lines. When the police ask you not to leave the country, it can mean only one thing."

His words resonated with Lacey. She thought back to that chilly evening on the island, as she was sat on her boulder with a man lying dead in the police's white tent. Superintendent Turner had asked her not to leave town. She'd known instinctively what that meant; that she was a suspect.

"They zeroed in on the outsider," she said, with a sudden surge of empathy.

Xavier nodded slowly. "It looks to be that way."

Lacey shouldn't have been surprised—the same thing had happened to her after Iris's death, too—but it still made her stomach feel heavy with sadness. It was as if the police automatically suspected the out-of-towner, as if they were unwilling to believe one of Wilfordshire's own could be the culprit.

Lacey's gaze flicked over to the inn. "No wonder you've been keeping out of the way."

"Yes, I am stuck here until this mess is sorted," Xavier confirmed. "I only stepped outside for some fresh air because I knew the rain would clear the streets."

That didn't stop him, for the hundredth time, from glancing around him. He was clearly on high alert, and Lacey couldn't help but feel terrible for him.

"This might sound crazy," Xavier added, "but I think I am under surveillance."

"It doesn't sound crazy at all," Lacey assured him, recalling how plain-clothes police had been stationed outside her store after Iris's death.

And though the streets were completely empty on account of the gray clouds and threat of rain, that didn't mean the police hadn't positioned people inside the surrounding buildings, watching from the window in order to report back that their main suspect was on the move. Lacey shuddered as she remembered just how invasive and disconcerting it had felt when she'd gone through the same thing.

"Can you help me?" Xavier said, suddenly.

"Me?" Lacey asked, taken aback. "Help you with what?"

"The police. The locals. I am stuck in a nightmare!"

"I don't know what I can do to help," Lacey said. "I'm in hot water with the police myself."

"Then we are in the same boat, are we not?" Xavier said. "You and I, we must stick together."

The sincerity in his tone was unmistakable, and the fact that he was appealing to her through their shared experience was compelling. But Lacey knew she mustn't let her personal experience cloud her judgment. Just because she saw something of her own experience in Xavier's didn't mean he was totally innocent. There were some weird coincidences connecting him with Buck's death; he'd gone head-to-head with Buck for the sextant, and been beaten. He was meant to be 30,000 feet in the air on a flight bound for Spain at the time of the murder, but was not. Lacey had to accept the very real possibility that she was standing face to face with Buck's killer.

But on the other hand, this was too good an opportunity to miss. If Xavier did have anything to do with the murder, this would be her only opportunity to question him. This was her chance to get him to divulge.

She looked down at Chester beside her. Her guard dog would keep her safe from harm.

Then she looked back up at Xavier. "I know somewhere quiet we can go and talk."

They walked side by side, quick-step, heads bowed against the drizzle and prying eyes. Lacey wasn't sure if she was behaving recklessly or not, but she'd chosen her path and she was sticking with it.

She was taking Xavier to Brooke's tearoom.

Though her preference was the patisserie, going there would've involved walking the entire length of the high street where they were bound to be spotted. The locals would lose their minds if they saw Lacey with Xavier, and she could kiss her reputation in this place goodbye forever. Besides, Tom had made it perfectly clear that he had no time for her at the moment. So she'd decided on Brooke's tearoom instead. It was in the other direction, away from the high street and along the seafront where the only other stores were touristy gift shops and arcades, all of which were closed on weekdays. And though Brooke's tearoom may be in a prime location on a sunny day, on a drizzly day no one really went to the beach, and most people decided not to venture too far from town.

It baffled Lacey a little bit; considering it rained so often in England, she'd have thought they'd be used to it, but she was quite certain if they went to Brooke's, they'd be the only people there. She'd also have an ally to witness the meeting, and a much needed dose of caffeine.

"It's just up here," she told Xavier, gesturing with her arm along the promenade.

Xavier took directions without question, following her like a lost lamb in desperate need of guidance.

Lacey felt her heart pounding with nerves as they marched along the promenade and up to the tearoom, triggering its automatic doors to swish open. Lacey went in first—a blast of air conditioning warming her instantly—with Xavier bringing up the rear.

"Well, if isn't my old mate, Lacey!" came Brooke's familiar, chipper voice. "And is that Tom?"

But when Xavier raised his head, Brooke blinked with surprise. Her gaze darted to Lacey, and her eyes filled with curiosity.

"This is Xavier," Lacey said, feeling odd to be introducing the man whom she'd only just learned the name of. "He's a contact of mine from the antiques world."

"I know who he is alright," Brooke said, stowing her cleaning rag at her hip. "He's the fella from the auction. The one who was bidding furiously on the sextant that a soon-to-be murdered man won!" She narrowed her eyes suspiciously and folded her arms in a hostile gesture.

Lacey bristled at her brazenness.

"I had nothing to do with Buck's death," Xavier said, holding both his hands up in a truce stance.

Lacey turned to him quickly, jumping in before Brooke had a chance to respond. "Go and take a seat," she said firmly out the side of her mouth. "I'll get the coffees."

Xavier cast a morose look toward Brooke, then finally acquiesced to Lacey's suggestion.

"Black. Thank you," he muttered, before slinking off past the cactuses and slumping down at one of the shabby chic picnic benches.

As soon as he was out of earshot, Lacey turned back to Brooke behind the counter and glared at her.

"You don't have to be so rude," Lacey said.

Brooke folded her arms. "What are you doing having coffee with a murder suspect!"

"Brooke, please," Lacey said, keeping her voice low in an attempt to encourage Brooke to lower her own. She had no such luck.

"You're being naive!" Brooke replied, loudly. "What happened? Did he sweet talk you with his Spanish charms? I thought you were smarter than that!"

Lacey frowned, displeased with Brooke's insinuation.

"Look," she said, firmly. "I'm doing my own investigation, okay? Xavier isn't the only suspect on the police's radar. I'm one too."

"You?" Brooke relied, looking like nothing could be more ludicrous.

"Yes," Lacey hissed. "The sextant was found in my store."

"So what?"

"So the police think I killed Buck to steal it back."

Brooke's eyes began to widen as realization dawned on her. "But ... but that makes *no* sense," she said, looking horrified.

"I know that. But the police think the sextant and the murder are connected."

She thought of her Venn diagram, with the MO for murder circle and the MO for theft circle, and that all important overlapping section in the middle. Just as she had in the beginning, the police would be focusing on the overlap. When she'd started her investigation earlier, the middle section only had Daisy's name in it. Now, a new name could be added: Xavier. But there was a third name, too, one that had belonged there all along: Lacey.

"That's so unfair," Brooke said, looking genuinely upset. Her gaze went past Lacey's shoulder to Xavier, who was sitting in a dejected slump. "But you don't actually think he's innocent, do you? He's the only other person who bid on the sextant..."

"I know," Lacey returned. "But if he wanted the sextant so bad he'd kill a man for it, then why the heck would he put it back in my store?"

Brooke looked stumped. She held her hands up in truce. "Alright, fine. You've got me. I don't know. I guess I'll just make you coffee like a good little barista. But if anything bad happens, I reserve the right to say I told you so."

She was only half joking, Lacey could tell.

She let her friend go off to make the coffees, and joined Xavier at his bench.

"Your barista friend thinks I did it," he said, as the sound of the coffee machine whirred to life in the background.

"She's just looking out for me," Lacey replied.

Chester settled himself beneath the picnic bench, but Lacey noticed that he wasn't relaxing. His ears were up, alert, taking in all the noises. His nose was lifted, sniffing for clues. Chester being on edge always put Lacey on edge as well. His doggy sixth sense had not failed her yet.

"But this is the thing, Lacey," Xavier began. "I . . . I do know something."

Lacey's stomach began to churn. "What do you know?"

"I know who is the murderer," he replied. "I saw them."

Lacey gasped. "What? When? Who is it?"

"I did not know what I was witnessing at the time," Xavier said, running his hands through his hair nervously. He let a beat pass, then announced, "But I was on the beach that night."

Lacey could feel the cogs in her mind beginning turn at a rate of knots. Xavier wasn't just in Wilfordshire at the time of the murder, he was practically at the scene! She held her tongue and listened as his explanation unfolded.

"I realized I was going to miss my flight almost as soon as I left the auction. The bidding had gone on much longer than I thought it would; I was so caught up in the moment I had not even noticed the time slip by. I left and called the airline to ask for a transfer. Well, of course it was a budget airline and you know how terrible they are; they refused and said I must pay for a whole new ticket! There was no space on a flight until the next morning, so I decided to stay in Wilfordshire for the night. What a bad choice I made. If I had just gone to the airport and stayed in an ugly hotel, none of this would have happened! But no, I decided to stay here, to be beside the ocean! *Estúpido!*"

"You're not stupid," Lacey told him. "You couldn't have known."

Xavier sank his head into his hands, and Lacey could see the expression of deep regret in his eyes. It was the look of missed opportunity, of hindsight, of one of those knife-edge moments in life where just one decision decides your fate forever.

Xavier exhaled loudly. "I booked myself a room at the Coach House Inn. I did one, two hours of work, maybe a little more, just catching up on emails. After that, I went for a long walk along the beach, heading west. I passed the island, and did not think much of it. But after I turned back—the light was fading, you see—that was when I saw the path of sand leading to the island. I was surprised; it had not been there before! So I paused, watching the tide come in, watching the water cover it. And that was when I saw the rowboat coming to shore."

Lacey continued listening without interruption, but her mind was in over-drive. Xavier was dropping in an excessive amount of extraneous information to his explanation. And if the sandbar had been out on his return trip, it must have been around seven p.m. But one or two hours of work would've taken him to 4 p.m., or 4:30 if she was being generous over how long it took him to check in at the inn. So he would have had to have been walking for three hours for the timing to match up. In his smart suit and leather brogues, no less, which were notoriously badly suited for walking on sand.

"I did not think much of the boat at first," Xavier continued. "Fishing is popular where I come from. Doing it during the quiet, dark hours is also very common. But then I heard her weeping."

"*Her?*" Lacey asked, interrupting him for the first time.

Xavier nodded, slowly. "*Her,*" he repeated. A moment of silence passed before he finished. "It was the wife."

Lacey was about to exclaim in shock, but Brooke suddenly appeared beside her, holding her tray of coffees and a bowl of doggy kibble for Chester. Lacey instantly snapped her lips shut, not wanting to say anything that might provoke Brooke into a scathing attack on Xavier.

Her friend must have noticed the descent of silence her presence had prompted, because she plonked the coffee down quite aggressively.

"Don't let me interrupt you," Brooke said, bending down to give Chester his bowl and a scratch before straightening back up, the silver tray dangling at her side, looking suspiciously from one silent companion to the next. "Jeez," she said, sounding quite offended now. "I'll leave you to your little murder mystery chat, shall I?"

Lacey watched Brooke walk away, feeling terrible about excluding her. But for whatever reason, Xavier trusted her, and she didn't know if he'd clam up if Brooke joined them. She made a note to apologize to her new friend later, once this was all over.

She went back to the conversation at hand, leaning closer to Xavier and keeping her voice down. "Are you sure it was Daisy you saw?"

Xavier nodded again. "I am certain. I could not see her face, no, only her hair, but I am confident it was her. I did not know then that she had come in from the island where Buck was found dead. I just thought it was odd that a woman was rowing a boat alone in the darkness, weeping."

"Did you tell the police what you saw?" she asked.

Xavier stared down into his coffee, looking guilty. "I did not. I thought it would make me look even more suspicious than I already did. It looked bad enough that I was not on my flight, but to say I was practically at the place of the murder was far, far worse."

Though Lacey understood his predicament, she couldn't agree with his actions. "If you don't tell the police what you saw, they won't be able to solve the crime. Your information could exonerate the both of us."

Xavier frowned in reaction to her harsh tone. "You think the police will believe me? The Coach House Inn was full when I left. Full of witnesses who saw me exiting the place at a time consistent with the man's murder!" He thumped his fist down on the tabletop. "I wish I had never come to your auction. *Estúpido!*"

"Then why did you?" Lacey asked, feeling suddenly affronted. There was no need to take this out on her. Especially since she was the only person in the whole town not declaring him a murderer.

"Because I am on a personal quest, trying to reunite all of my *abuelo's* antiques. That is to say, my mother's great-grandfather. *Abuelo* was a famous ship captain, and had a whole trove of relics that were passed down as family heirlooms. Then we discovered *papá* had been quietly selling everything to pay for his mistress. Mamá was devastated, as you can imagine, and I promised her I'd track them all down and bring them home. I managed to trace a substantial portion of them to America, to a store in New York called Doyle's."

Lacey gasped. Her hand flew to her mouth.

"That was my father's store," she said, her voice almost a squeak.

Xavier looked stunned. "Really? When I saw there was another Doyle's Antiques in England, I thought it was a chain. But . . . you mean, you are related?"

"I'm his daughter," Lacey said. Her throat felt very tight now and she was tearing up. "And I found the sextant by complete chance in the local charity shop."

Was it all just a coincidence? That two of Xavier's great-great-grandfather's relics, that had traveled to different parts of the globe, could be connected by her father? Or perhaps he'd purchased all the relics when he was in Wilfordshire on vacation, and accidentally left the sextant behind? That would explain how it ended up on a shelf of novelty mugs in the local charity shop, but it didn't feel satisfying to her. Her father wasn't careless. She couldn't imagine him leaving an item like the sextant behind accidentally. She could only picture him giving it to someone as a gift.

Lacey couldn't help herself. Her mind began wandering back to the past, and that last vacation she'd spent with her parents as a married couple in Wilfordshire. There'd been an antiques store, she could remember shopping in it. There'd been a figurine, that Naomi broke accidentally, cutting her finger. And then there'd been the woman. The beautiful woman whom Lacey still had flashes of memories of. Was there a chance *she* had been the recipient of the sextant? Had her father gifted it to her, only for it to find its way to the local charity store years later?

Lacey desperately wanted to ask Xavier to tell her everything about his trip to her father's store, but at that very moment, a figure appeared at her left shoulder. She turned, expecting to see Brooke, but was surprised to discover that it was Superintendent Turner standing over her.

"Xavier Santino," the detective announced, "I'm arresting you on suspicion of the murder of Buckland Stringer."

Xavier's face crumbled. Lacey looked past Superintendent Turner to the counter Brooke was standing behind. The look on her face told Lacey everything she needed to know. Brooke had called the police and tipped them off.

"You do not have to say anything," Superintendent Turner continued. "But it may harm your defense if you do not mention when questioned something which you later rely on in court. Anything you do say may be given in evidence."

Lacey's mind swirled. She couldn't believe what was happening. She stared, dumbfounded, as Xavier was cuffed.

But then she saw that DCI Lewis was heading right for her, and her disbelief magnified tenfold.

"Miss Doyle, I'm afraid I'm going to have to arrest you too," the female detective said.

"What?" Lacey cried, leaping up. "Why? I haven't done anything!"

At her sudden movement, Chester began barking.

Brooke suddenly yelped. She caught Lacey's eyes and deep regret flashed in her expression as she realized calling in her suspicions to the police had landed her innocent friend in trouble.

"Someone get that dog under control," Superintendent Turner commanded.

Brooke scurried to the dog and took him by the collar.

"I'm so sorry, Lacey," she said. "I didn't mean for this to happen."

With Chester under control, DCI Lewis took Lacey by her right arm.

"Lacey Doyle, I'm arresting you on suspicion of aiding and abetting, perverting the course of justice, and withholding information from police."

Lacey was too stunned to do anything, and allowed the detective to guide her left hand toward her right, and cuff them together at the wrist.

"You do not have to say anything," DCI Lewis continued, "But it may harm your defense if you do not mention when questioned something which you later rely on in court. Anything you do say may be given in evidence."

Her words faded in Lacey's ears. The whole world seemed to lag as she was led toward the automatic doors. She turned back to a horrified-looking Brooke, her hand still clutching Chester's collar as the dog barked frantically.

"I'm sorry, Lacey!" Brooke cried. "I'll put this right. I'm sorry!"

Lacey's mind swirled as DCI Lewis guided her to the second of two police cruisers parked on the promenade. She passed Xavier, who was being helped him into the back of his car by Superintendent Turner, with one hand on his head, just like in the movies. She'd seen this scene before on the big screen but never in real life.

And then it was her turn. The detective opened the back door and gestured for her to enter into the darkness.

She did, thudding into the backseat, her mind spinning with confusion. It smelled too clean in the car, like chemicals. It all added to Lacey's disorientation, which was furthered by the drizzle covered windows. She peered out at the streets, feeling as if she was seeing them from an entirely new perspective. Her whole town felt suddenly unfamiliar.

From the car ahead, Superintendent Turner began to pull away from the curb. Detective Lewis started the engine of her car, following him out.

Lacey stared behind her at the tearoom.

Just then, the automatic doors swished open. She was expecting to see Brooke, but instead, it was Chester who appeared. He came flying out and onto the sidewalk.

"My dog!" Lacey cried, putting her cuffed hands up to the windows. "You have to pull over. My dog's got loose."

She quickly looked at DCI Lewis in the driver's seat. The woman pulled her lips into a thin line, and shook her head, clearly unmoved by Lacey's plight.

Lacey swirled back to the rear window.

Brooke had appeared, coming out of the tearoom and chasing after Chester. But she was no match for the dog. Lacey had never seen Chester run so fast. He was going faster than he even had when he'd bolted across the sandbar.

As the cruiser gained speed, Chester shrank smaller and smaller, until he was nothing but a dot on the horizon.

Lacey turned back around and let her tears fall.

CHAPTER FOURTEEN

Lacey had never seen the inside of the police station before. Even after everything that had happened before with Iris' murder and her being the police's prime suspect, it had never gotten so far as for her to be taken into one of their interrogation rooms.

It was small in here. There were no windows, just horrible fluorescent strip lights that buzzed and gave her a headache. The only furniture was the chair she was sitting upon, another (currently vacant) chair for the police officer, and a small table, all squished in in a way to deliberately make her uncomfortable. The red light of a CCTV camera blinked in the corner of the room, reminding her that she was being watched. Her hands shook on her lap, where they were still clasped together with the strange plastic cuffs, the sight of which reminded her she was in a foreign jail far away from home. Somehow, that made it even worse.

Lacey had no idea how long she'd been sitting here waiting. She'd seen enough true crime shows to know it was a police tactic. The longer you were left waiting, the longer you had to stew, and more rattled you'd be when they did finally get around to speaking to you.

It was a pretty effective tactic, Lacey learned. It didn't take long for her to begin ruminating on all the ills of the day, from Tom not having time for her to Brooke stupidly calling the police on Xavier.

No, it wasn't stupid, Lacey scolded herself.

Brooke had obviously panicked. She must have genuinely thought Xavier was a murderer and decided to call time on him casually sitting in her tearoom drinking coffee. She may well have thought they were in danger. But she was naive to have thought the police would only arrest Xavier. And after Lacey had *told* her she was a suspect!

She sighed heavily and her shoulders slumped forward.

And then there was Chester...

Yes, Lacey knew that the dog had been frantic, that he'd been straining against Brooke's hold. But couldn't she have put him in the back room? Instead she must have lost hold of the poor creature. Lacey could only hope that Chester was okay, that Brooke had caught up to him and called Gina to pick him up, or had taken him to the patisserie to be with Tom. But what if she hadn't? What if Chester was lost?

The thought was too horrible to entertain. It made Lacey's stomach ache.

Just then, the door opened with a loud creak, making Lacey start. Superintendent Turner came in.

Lacey tensed. She'd been hoping for Beth. She always seemed the more reasonable to the pair.

"Miss Doyle," Karl Turner said, in his lazy seen-it-all-before voice. He sank into the seat opposite her and dropped a thick pile of papers onto the desk, where they landed with a *thwop*.

"Hello, Detective," she replied coldly.

If it weren't for the fact that she'd been arrested, Lacey might have found some humor in the situation. She'd had so many run-ins with the detective now, he felt like something of an acquaintance. Seeing him in interrogator mode was a little comical. It was as if he'd slipped on a badly fitting mask.

He leaned forward, elbows on knees, closing the gap between them. It was the closest he'd come to her since that incident last month when he'd lost his cool and pointed his finger right in her face. She hadn't noticed then—perhaps because of how terrifying and out of the blue his blow-up had been—that he had the grayest irises she'd ever seen.

"Lacey Doyle," he said, shaking his head as if her name alone was a source of irritation. "Wilfordshire's very own Sherlock Holmes. This must be rather exciting for you, getting a behind the scenes look."

Lacey pressed her back into the chair rest, trying to get as much space between her and the detective as possible.

Don't let him get under your skin, she told herself.

But that was easier said than done.

"I can assure you it's far from exciting," she said, calmly. "Being led in handcuffs to a police vehicle while my dog runs loose isn't my idea of fun."

He smirked. Clearly he couldn't care less about the dog's well-being.

"When do I get my phone call?" Lacey said. "I need to know if Chester's okay."

This time, Superintendent Turner's smirk turned into a condescending sneer. "You'd waste your phone call checking up on the dog? Rather than, I don't know, calling a lawyer?"

He had such a patriarchal tone in his voice, Lacey felt herself bristle. She clenched her teeth tightly together. Any thoughts she'd had about this being humorous disappeared.

"So," Karl said, picking up his notes and leafing through them. "I'm wondering what theory you've come up with. You're always so full of ideas."

"Are you asking me to do your job for you, Superintendent?" Lacey replied without missing a beat.

Karl's face remained unmoved. "Okay. How about I start? Here's what I think happened." He placed a pen on the desk. "This is Mrs. Stringer. We know that on the evening of Mr. Stringer's murder she was here, in Taryn's boutique." He moved the pen to the farthest end of the table. "And Mr. Stringer..." He put a bulldog clip on the table. "He was all the way over here." He slid it toward Lacey, before tapping it on the surface of the table a few times directly beneath her. "On the island. Dead." He put an eraser on the desk next, a grubby little rectangle that had once been white but was now gray with age. "Now we have Mr. Santino. Here. On the beach." Finally, he put an empty plastic cup—the type that came from a watercooler—next to the eraser. "And who do you think this represents?"

Lacey ground her teeth, knowing full well that Superintendent Turner was implying *she* was the second person on the beach that night, that for some reason she was working alongside Xavier, and that they'd committed the crime together.

She had to fight the urge to snarkily tell the detective that an ugly plastic water cooler cup wasn't particularly representative of her, because she knew he'd latch on to it as evidence of her placing herself at the scene.

"How interesting," the detective said, with faux curiosity. "Little Miss Mouthy has nothing to say? This must be a first. Don't worry, 'll answer for you." He tapped the cup. "This, Miss Doyle, is you. Standing beside Xavier Santino on the beach. He's just told you that he's done the job you hired him for. He's killed Buckland Stringer. Now you can keep the sextant, hang onto it until the heat dies down, and resell it. Two paydays. You split the money and go about your lives."

Lacey had never heard anything so preposterous. For starters, she'd only found out Xavier's name earlier that day, and had only just heard his surname now for the first time! Secondly, he looked so far from a hitman it was laughable. Hitmen didn't usually wear expensive designer suits and keep their facial hair neatly trimmed. Did they?

"You think I killed one of my customers?" Lacey said slowly, making sure her tone left no doubt just how ludicrous a suggestion it was. "So I could steal back the item I'd just sold them in order to sell it again?" She raised an eyebrow. "Now, you don't need a degree to know that's one heck of a terrible business model."

The detective narrowed his eyes. He obviously didn't like it when people used his own tactics back at him, but it was good for him to get a taste of his own medicine.

"I know all about how your business works," the detective hissed, jabbing his index finger on the stack of notes. "You take a 10% down payment on the day. The rest on delivery. But not this time. This time the transaction was for the full sum. Twenty-nine sales you made at that auction. A 10% down payment for every single item." He jabbed his finger along with the next three words, punctuating them. "Except. This. One. The sextant. The stolen sextant that reappeared in your store!"

Lacey shook her head. It certainly looked bad from an outsider's perspective. She knew she'd have to explain the inconsistency very carefully.

"Buck asked to pay in full and take the item away with him. In fact, he demanded it. I tried to get him to follow the usual protocol but he was adamant. There were dozens of witnesses. You can ask any one of them what happ—"

"Yes, we've spoken to most of the members of the English Antiques Society already," the detective said, cutting her off. "They all seemed to be in agreement that Mr. Stringer was a bit of a fish out of water in that auction room. He didn't know the usual protocols. The etiquette. He was inexperienced. Your friends at the society also all explained how there was a bidding war between Mr. Stringer and Mr. Santino, a man who, I'm sure you'd agree, was extremely familiar with the protocols, and who backed out of the race after driving the price up exponentially, to a point where all in attendance could see Mr. Stringer was sweating. Answer me this, Miss Doyle. Do your auctions usually go that way—with an expert pitted against a novice, one cool and calm, the other so stressed out by the whole thing as to be visibly sweating? Tell me, is it at all ethical to push a man to such extremes?"

Lacey couldn't hold it back any longer. It was one thing to throw a baseless hypothesis at her, but quite enough to insult her integrity and professionalism! Her frustration bubbled over.

"We have been through this before, Karl. If you recall, you were barking up the wrong tree that time as well! You ended up with egg on your face, having to display an actual written apology afterwards!

"That was Beth's idea," he said, shortly. "I'd never do anything so twee."

"Well, you'll have no choice once you realize how unfathomably incorrect you are right now. Your theory is full of holes. I would need to be as idiotic as you're being right now to think of hiding a stolen sextant on a shelf in plain view of everyone! Secondly, the sextant was an extremely rare item. It's not the sort of thing that can just be sold twice without someone noticing. My auction gathered together navel enthusiasts from across the whole country. Anyone and everyone who might have an interest in buying something was in attendance. If I attempted to sell the sextant again, you'd have about fifty people calling you up to say I was selling stolen goods!" She reached over and tapped the dossier of papers. "And I thought you said you'd read up all about how my business worked."

With triumph, she sat back in her chair and folded her arms.

Superintendent Turner looked like he'd sucked a lemon. But before he had the chance to utter a rebuttal, the door flew open so dramatically it slammed into the wall.

A woman marched in. She looked to be in her late sixties, the creases in her forehead and sagging purple bags beneath her eyes showing the signs of a busy, stressful lifestyle. But in her smart black suit she looked elegant, and the strawberry blond hair that hung to her shoulders was sleek and healthy.

"This interview must cease right away," the woman said.

"Who are you?" Superintendent Turner demanded. "You can't come barging in here! I'll have you arrested."

"I'm Miss Doyle's lawyer," the woman said. "And my client is being held as an accessory to murder, supposedly having worked in cahoots with a suspect who has not yet been charged with murder! You know the law as well as I do, Detective; you can only question my client as a witness. Which means your arrest was a charade, and my client is free to leave."

Lacey snapped her head to face Karl, stunned by what the woman was saying. But it was written all over his face. Her arrest was fake! He'd been trying to rattle her, to make her think she didn't have the right to walk right out of here when all along she did. And the cuffs! Surely cuffing a witness was illegal.

Lacey stood, filled with fury. "Now I'm actually lost for words."

"Don't worry, dear," the lawyer said. "I'll make sure we sue him for gross misconduct."

She whisked Lacey out of the room, slamming the door behind her so ferociously, the noise echoed through the corridor.

Everything had happened so fast, Lacey's head was spinning. She felt dizzy, and put her hand on the wall to steady herself as the lawyer practically dragged her down the corridor.

"I'm sorry, who are you?" Lacey finally asked. "I didn't request a lawyer."

"Well, that's your first mistake," the woman said bluntly, pausing at the door that led into the waiting room, and looking over her shoulder at Lacey. "Never speak to the police without a lawyer."

She heaved on the handle and ushered Lacey into the reception area.

Lacey blinked under the glare of yet more strip lights and took in the sight of shabby linoleum flooring and horrible plastic chairs. One was occupied by a shaven-headed man holding a cloth up to a bloody gash on his cheek, bright splatters of red on his jeans. Beside him, an anxious looking woman rung her hands in her lap. And beside *her*, much to Lacey's astonishment, was Tom.

He jumped up at the sight of her and ran to her.

Lacey was so stunned to see him she froze on the spot. He wrapped his arms around her. Then those familiar scents of pastry and ocean air overpowered the police station's cleaning fluid smell, and Lacey finally came to her senses. She wrapped her arms around him too.

"What are you doing here?" she squeaked with relief.

"Brooke called. She said you'd been arrested."

"So it was you who contacted the lawyer."

"Kinda," Tom replied in her ear. "Lacey, this is my mom, Heidi."

Lacey drew back and swirled to face the strawberry blond woman. "You're Mrs. Forrester?" she exclaimed. Then she looked at Tom, aghast, and hissed under her breath. "*This* is how you introduce me to your mother?"

He gave her a sheepish grin. How typical of Tom to not even consider how humiliating it would be for Lacey to meet his mother for the first time under these circumstances! It was hardly going to give off a good first impression.

"It will make a great anecdote one day," Heidi Forrester quipped.

She had the same sense of humor as her son, Lacey noted. *Must be where he gets it from.*

Just then, the double glass doors to the station opened and a man, clearly drunk, staggered in. He hiccupped and weaved his way past the group to the reception desk. The officer sitting on the other side of the bullet-proof screen glanced him up and down.

"Are you here to report a crime?"

"Yes," the man slurred, hiccupping again. "My keys aren't in my pocket."

He started pulling his pockets inside out, spewing credit cards and candy wrappers onto the floor.

"Is there a chance you dropped them?" the officer said dispassionately.

"No way," the inebriated man said confidently. "They've been stolen."

"Can we get out of here?" Tom said, turning away from the ensuing debate between police officer and drunk man about the difference between something being stolen and something being lost.

"What about Xavier?" Lacey said.

"Xavier?" Tom asked.

"The Spanish man, from my auction," she explained, realizing Tom had no idea what she'd been doing prior to her arrest, nor with whom she'd been doing it. "The one who lost out on the sextant to Buck. They arrested him as well, on suspicion of murder. We can't leave him in there." She looked at Heidi. "Can you help him?"

But before she replied, Tom shook his head and placed a hand on Lacey's arm. "I'm sure the police had a reason to arrest him."

"Like they did me?" Lacey returned, moving her arm out from under his hand. She huffed. "Xavier saw Daisy rowing back to shore on the night of the murder. He's not a suspect, he's a witness." She paused, recalling how Superintendent Turner had told her Daisy had an alibi. Had Xavier lied? Or had

Daisy? She shook her head, trying to get her thoughts back on track. "Anyway, he's in the same situation I was—a foreigner in a country with a different legal jurisdiction. We should help him."

But Tom's mom looked unmoved. "Sorry, there's just no grounds to help him on. No loophole to work in his case like there was yours."

"How long can they keep him here for?" Lacey asked.

"They have seventy-two hours before they either have to charge him or release him."

"Three days!" Lacey exclaimed.

To think if Tom hadn't had a lawyer for a mom, she more than likely would have spent the next three days locked inside a cell for something she hadn't done!

Lacey glanced back at the door that led to interrogation rooms, where she knew Xavier would be behind one being grilled. But there was nothing she could do to help him. Unless, of course, she looked into Daisy's alibi. If she could expose Daisy as a liar, then hopefully she'd be able to get Xavier out.

She left the station—and Xavier—behind her, vowing to uncover the truth once and for all.

CHAPTER FIFTEEN

Lacey hurried down the steps of the police station, discovering, for the first time, that she'd been inside the windowless interrogation room long enough for the sky to have turned black. But rather than lamenting her own misfortune, Lacey's concern was with her poor missing pooch. The image of him pelting down the street after the police kept repeating in her mind's eye like a horrible scene from a movie, and now she saw how late it really was, she felt even worse.

She turned to Tom, who was walking down the steps with his mother at a snail's pace.

"Did Brooke say anything about Chester when you spoke with her?" Lacey asked while he was still a few steps away.

"No," he said, taking the last steps and joining her on the sidewalk. "Why?"

"Because he was with me in the tearoom when I got arrested!" Lacey exclaimed, feeling her anguish take hold of her. "Brooke had him by the collar when they cuffed me, but he went berserk. He was so worried for me. You should've seen him." She felt tears welling in her eyes at the memory. "Then he must've got out of her hold because he started chasing the car down the street."

"Oh my," Heidi said, a hand covering her mouth.

Lacey chewed her bottom lip fretfully, her worry seeming to magnify now that she'd spoken it aloud.

"So Brooke didn't bring him to patisserie?" she questioned Tom.

Tom shook his head. "No, she didn't. When she came by to tell me about your arrest, she wasn't with him. She didn't even mention him, she was in such a state of panic about you." He reached out and rubbed her arm to comfort her. "Please don't worry. You know Chester. He'll find his way back home. In fact, I'd put money on him being there now, waiting for you."

He tried to smile reassuringly, but Lacey was having none of it.

"If he was going to go anywhere, it would be my store," she said. "It's more familiar to him than Crag Cottage, and he's gone there before on his own volition. I should go and check."

But before she had a chance to move, Tom took her by the shoulders, grounding her. "Lacey. If Chester was going to go to the store, I would've seen him on the high street already. It's a ten-minute walk max between the tearoom and your store."

"But he chased me over half the way along the promenade road," Lacey told him, hearing her voice becoming more frantic. "That's the opposite direction. And he was running full pelt. It could've easily taken him an hour to make it back."

"Or," Tom said, in his reassuring tone, "it could mean that he decided to head home. He's a smart dog. Once he saw the beach, he probably worked out it would take him home. All he'd have to do was follow the coast until he reached the cliff path up to your house. That's how animals' brains work. We had a cat that did that once. Remember, Mom?"

He turned to Heidi. The strawberry blond had been waiting patiently while they hashed the situation out, but she'd taken a little step apart from them and her gaze was now averted. At the sound of her son's attempts to include her, she smiled attentively.

"That's right. Pickles. She'd follow the canal path for miles."

Lacey couldn't stop herself. "Yes, but Chester isn't a cat."

Her tone was snipey. If she'd been worried about making a terrible first impression to Heidi before, she'd more or less blown it now.

Tom rubbed her arm again, though it felt to Lacey like he was handling her with kid gloves.

"You're right," he said. "Chester's *way* smarter than a cat. He'll be back at Crag Cottage. Mark my words. We should all head there. Have a cup of tea. I'll cook something to eat, since we've missed dinner."

There was no debating, Lacey realized. Tom, as the rescuer and getaway driver, had taken command. And he was obviously also thinking with his stomach; Tom wasn't one for missing a meal.

"Fine," Lacey muttered, realizing there was no way arguing.

"Great!" Tom said, as if she'd actually had a choice in the matter. He looked over at his mother again. "What do you say?"

Heidi smiled. She had the same genial, genuine smile as her son. "That sounds lovely. As long as Lacey doesn't mind?"

The last thing Lacey felt like doing was sitting down and having a nice cup of tea with her new boyfriend's mother. What Lacey wanted to do was find her poor dog who'd gone MIA, then head to Taryn's boutique to carry on with her investigations. Taryn had given Daisy an alibi for the time that Xavier sighted her on the beach. The two events were in complete contradiction. Either Taryn was lying, or Xavier was. If she could put the alibi to the test herself, she'd be one step closer to finding out the truth.

But as much as she wanted to dive right back into the detective work, Tom had made a good point about Chester. He'd managed to make his way back to the store after the car crash that killed his prior owners, after all, and that journey had taken him days. He clearly had a very strong homing instinct, and the likelihood of him being at Crag Cottage waiting for her was quite high.

So she nodded, and returned Heidi's and Tom's twin smiles.

"I don't mind at all," she said.

As grateful as Lacey was for Tom swooping in and saving the day, she felt extremely uncomfortable in the back seat of his van, as he drove both her and his mother across town toward the cliffs. She was hardly in the right frame of mind to make a good impression.

"How are you enjoying living in Wilfordshire?" Heidi asked. "Tom says you recently moved from New York City. It must be quite a change for you."

Small talk, Lacey thought with dread. That was about the last thing she felt like doing right now.

"I love it," Lacey said. "The sea. The people. It's been a lovely change of pace."

If only it hadn't been for all the murders, she thought wryly.

They reached Crag Cottage and Tom pulled up in the driveway.

"This is your house?" Heidi asked. "It's charming."

"Thanks," Lacey said, still unable to relax into conversation.

She headed up the garden path. The front door to Crag Cottage opened before she got there. Gina was standing there on her porch.

"Gina?" Lacey exclaimed. "What are you doing here? Is it Chester? Did he come home?"

Gina shook her head. "No, I'm sorry poppet. Brooke told me what happened. She was in a right state about it, feeling really guilty about everything. But I told her the same thing I'm going to tell you; Chester has a strong homing instinct, he will find his way home sooner or later."

"Let's hope sooner," Lacey said, feeling morose.

Gina took her in her arms for a comforting embrace. "I've called the vet to let her know, and I've also logged him missing with the microchip company. If only those chips had GPS, eh?"

Gina released her, and Lacey let out a sad smile.

"Now, come in out of the drizzle," Gina said. "I'll get the kettle on."

Against all the motherly instinct telling her to run off in search of her missing pet, Lacey felt an even stronger pull coming from Gina, and so she went inside her home.

"It's Heidi, isn't it?" Gina said to Tom's mother as they strolled through the corridor.

"Yes, that's right," Mrs. Forrester replied. "Have we met?"

"Once or twice," Gina told her.

"I'm sorry. I meet so many people in my field of work."

Gina chuckled. "Colorful types, I imagine."

Lacey felt out of place as she listened to their chitchat. She was in her own home, and yet she felt as if she was the guest!

Gina went straight for the kettle to make tea, Tom to the fridge to make dinner. Lacey slumped at the butcher's block table and let it all happen around her. The clinking of crockery. The whooshing kettle. The merry chitchat as the three of them engaged in friendly small talk as if they had no cares in the world. Lacey felt unable to join in. Everything swirled around her. Her mind couldn't settle her mind. She'd lost Chester. She'd spent a day in an interrogation room. And Xavier was still inside.

The moist nuzzling of Boudica's nose against her arm was the final straw for Lacey. She stood, abruptly, making her stool squeak against the tiles.

Everyone stopped and turned to look at her.

"Lacey?" Tom asked. "Is everything okay?"

She shook her head. "I can't do this. I can't sit here pretending everything's fine. I need to look for Chester." She rubbed her pounding head as her swirling thoughts turned into a tornado in her mind. "I need to *do* something."

"What you need is a warm meal in your stomach," Gina said. "And a long sleep."

"Sleep?" Lacey exclaimed. "My dog is out there somewhere, wandering the streets. The same streets a murderer is currently walking, might I add!"

An awkward silence filled the room. Lacey squirmed as three pairs of eyes blinked at her with expressions ranging from sympathy to bemusement.

Heidi spoke. "Lacey, in all probability, the murderer is the man sitting in the police station."

"Xavier didn't do this," Lacey returned.

Tom quirked his head to the side. "How can you be so certain? He has the clearest motive. He wanted the sextant so bad he killed for it."

"And he had the opportunity," Heidi added.

Lacey narrowed her eyes and shook her head. "No. No way. If Xavier killed Buck for the sextant, then why would he have put it in my store?"

"He couldn't exactly keep it on him, could he?" Tom said.

"And if the police picked him up at six a.m.," Heidi continued, "and prevented him from leaving the country, he must've realized he needed to hide the sextant somewhere safe. Well, where would be safer than back where it had originally been?"

Lacey looked from mother to son, watching them get caught up in their hypothesis.

"Your store was the only other place in Wilfordshire he was familiar with," Gina said, adding her theory to the fray. "Perhaps he went straight there hoping to see you, so he could slip it in with your items when you weren't looking? But he found the back door open." She coughed into her fist with embarrassment. "So he decided just to put it inside."

Tom immediately latched onto Gina's embellishment, adding to it with his own. "Yes! I bet that whole thing about your dad's store was just a cover story he had prepared so that when you asked him why he was back at the antiques store he'd have something to tell you!"

He looked as animated as the other two. The three amigos who thought they'd solved a crime. But Lacey wasn't sharing in their enthusiasm one bit. She'd listened to them all, feeling more and more frustrated.

She folded her arms. "And what about the fact he saw Daisy on the beach that night? Rowing a boat! How does that fit in with your theory?"

The three exchanged glances. It was Heidi who answered, using a gentle tone as if she didn't want to make Lacey feel stupid.

"He's lying. In fact, that might even be an embedded confession. He's placed himself almost exactly at the scene of the crime. He's given an explanation as to how he got on and off the island."

Lacey had heard enough. She headed for the back door.

"Lacey?" Tom said, looking a bit perturbed. "What are you doing?"

"I already told you," she said, reaching for her rain mac. The drizzle from earlier was still lingering in the air, and Lacey didn't want to risk it. "I'm going to look for Chester."

Tom hurried over to her. He spoke in a stage whisper. "My mother is here. We're in *your* house. You can't just leave."

Lacey looked over his shoulder at Heidi. She was wearing the same slightly perturbed expression as Tom. She was probably wondering what on earth her son saw in this lunatic of a woman. But there were far more important matters at hand than making a good impression.

"I'm sorry, Mrs. Forrester. You just caught me at a bad time. I hope next time we meet, it will be under better circumstances."

She pulled open the back door and hurried out, not wanting to see the look of disapproval she was sure was now on Tom's face.

CHAPTER SIXTEEN

Lacey tried to temper her fury as she sped down the cliff road in her second-hand Volvo. She should never have let Tom talk her into going back to Crag Cottage. She should have insisted they head out in search of Chester right away!

Lacey turned onto the high street, glancing at the Coach House Inn, the center of all gossip, as she went. She wondered what conversations they were having inside. By now, they would have all heard about her and Xavier's arrests. They probably had concocted a million wild theories about the pair of them. They probably sounded just like Tom and Heidi and Gina earlier, as they threw around accusations as carelessly as confetti!

Lacey parked up outside her store, throwing her champagne colored Volvo onto the curb.

'Gina actually locked up properly for once,' she thought as she climbed out, noting that the shutters of her store had been pulled down securely.

There was no sign of Chester on the street outside the store, so Lacey decided to try round the back. She went around to the side gate—which Gina had also miraculously locked properly—and into the garden.

"Chester?" she called. "Are you here?"

She checked to see if he was sheltering in the greenhouse or shed, which would be warm on this chilly spring evening. Both were empty.

The pit of worry in her guts grew even stronger. Where could the poor pup have gone?

She was just about to head back inside when she noticed there was a light on in the boutique's back room. Taryn must be working late. Maybe she'd seen Chester?

I can test Daisy's alibi while I'm at it, Lacey thought, as she stepped over the knee-high fence that separated their yards.

She went up to Taryn's patio doors. Inside, she could see Taryn amongst the stock in the back room, organizing things. She rapped her knuckles against the glass.

Taryn leaped a mile. Then a scowl came over her features and she marched over, unlocking the door and heaving it so hard it slid on its runners, hit the doorstop, and almost bounced closed again.

"What the hell are you doing?" Taryn screeched. "Are you trying to give me a heart attack? Who the hell lurks around in the dark like that! And you know how much I've been freaking out about the footpath back there, and burglars."

As she spoke, Lacey noticed the CCTV camera in the corner of the store, blinking away. State of the art, Superintendent Turner had said. HD quality. She wondered if the machine really did hold footage that provided Daisy with an alibi. If it did, that would prove Xavier was a liar. And if he lied about seeing Daisy on the beach, then that begged the question, what else had he lied about?

"Have you seen Chester?" Lacey asked, ignoring her tirade.

Taryn's frown only deepened. "Why would I have seen your stinking dog?"

"Because he ran off and I thought he might've come here, maybe gotten around into the gardens for shelter. You've been working late, right? So, have you seen him at all?"

"No," Taryn snapped. "I haven't. And by the way, if your dog so much as sets foot on my grass I'll have a wall built between our gardens. That you pay for. I am not having a disgusting dog poop on my property, or make muddy paw prints in the grass. Or ... Lacey? Hello, earth to Lacey? What are you staring at?" She looked over her shoulder, then back again, her expression even more nonplussed. "Are you staring at my CCTV camera?"

Lacey finally fixed her gaze back on Taryn, the vast majority of her rant having passed her by.

"Can I ask you something?" Lacey said.

"Now?" Taryn replied haughtily. "Can it wait? It's already really late and I'm only halfway through organizing everything back here."

"Let me help," Lacey said.

Anything to get Taryn to speak.

Taryn folded her arms. "You want to help me? Why? Whatever you want to talk to me about must be very important." Suddenly, her eyes sparked with excitement. "Is it about Tom? Have you had a fight?" A look of malevolent glee lit up her entire face. "Did you break up?"

"It's about Daisy," Lacey said.

The excitement faded from Taryn's face. "What about her?"

"I heard you were her alibi."

Taryn sighed loudly. "Alright. Come in. This is obviously going to take forever. I may as well get some free labor out of it."

Lacey placed the armful of gray silk blouses on the counter and began folding them as per Taryn's instructions. While she folded, the boutique owner worked through her own pile, relaying the story of the night Daisy had been in her store.

"She was in here for literally hours," Taryn said. "A total pain in the ass. She asked for the full stylist experience, then rejected all of my suggestions! Basically, if it wasn't pink, she wasn't interested."

Lacey looked down at the array of grays and beiges in her stack. Pink wasn't the sort of color Taryn stocked. It only added to her curiosity as to why Daisy would pick the boutique to shop in, when it didn't sell anything she particularly liked, and if she was only going to reject the expert she'd come for the opinion of.

"Do you even stock pink?" Lacey asked.

"Luckily, I had some stuff left over from last season," Taryn replied. "In that dusky pink color that everyone went crazy for about five minutes. You should know the one I mean, you have a sweater in that color. Anyway, I had about five dresses, a pair of heels, and a couple of leather handbags in the same color that didn't shift in the end of season sale. She loved them. Even the halter dress that anyone with breasts over a C-cup know is an absolute fashion no-no!" She sighed. "Some people can't even buy style."

Taryn herself was one of those rake-thin fashionistas without a hint of a curve. Today, she was wearing her signature little black dress, only this one had a plunging neckline that showed off her bony, breastless chest. She and Daisy were at the opposite ends of the style spectrum.

"Did she buy anything?" Lacey asked, thinking about the unpaid bills the other vendors on the street had ended up with.

"Yes, eventually. Five dresses, a pair of heels and a handbag. All in the same color." She scoffed.

Lacey couldn't help but think that Taryn's disdain was uncalled for. No matter how annoying Daisy might have been during her stay in Wilfordshire, it was still uncalled for.

"How long was Daisy in here?" Lacey asked, trying to keep Taryn focused on the night in question.

"It seemed like forever. She was rude. Arrogant. I had to keep the store open well past closing time."

"How late?" Lacey pressed.

Taryn whistled. "I dunno. Six? Seven? Something like that."

Lacey wondered if the police had double-checked the times on the security footage, or if they'd just relied on Daisy and Taryn's statements. People were notoriously bad at keeping track of the time, and Taryn might've accidentally exaggerated how long Daisy was in the store because it *felt* long. And Daisy obviously would've exaggerated how long *she* was in the store because it gave her an alibi. The difference between her leaving at six and her leaving at seven could be the difference in her having the window of opportunity to commit murder or not.

Working on the assumption that the police had corroborated the statements with the security camera footage clocks, then that would mean that Daisy wasn't the killer, and Xavier had invented his sighting of her on the beach that night. Which made it even more likely that he was the killer. But then why return the sextant to her store? Could it really have played out the way Heidi, Gina and Tom imagined it had, that he knew the police would search him and had hidden the sextant in the only place he could think of?

"Lacey!" Taryn exclaimed, breaking through her ruminations. "Careful!"

Lacey looked down. She'd been so caught up in her thoughts, her entire pile of folded silk blouses had slid to the floor.

When Lacey returned home, without Chester, exhausted and overwhelmed, she found a note on the kitchen counter. It was in Gina's handwriting.

I hope we didn't upset you earlier. Tom made quiche. There's some in the fridge. Try to eat and get some sleep. I'm coming over at sunrise. We can look for Chester together.

Lacey smiled sadly and opened the fridge door. Tom had made his sundried tomato, goats cheese and pesto quiche, and half of it was left. Lacey grabbed the plate from the fridge and a clean fork from the utensils drawer, then took the entire lot upstairs into her bedroom. She quickly changed out of her clothes before getting into bed and tucking into the quiche. It tasted divine, but it didn't comfort her as much as the feeling of Chester lying on her feet would. The bed felt too big and empty without him in it.

"Please come home," she whispered to the space he should be in, as a tear streaked down her cheek.

CHAPTER SEVENTEEN

Knock-knock-knock.

Lacey awoke with a start. She sat up, disorientated. It was barely daybreak, and everything was bathed in gray light.

Lacey looked around her bedroom, trying to orient herself. She was in bed. A plate covered in crumbs lay on the pillow beside her. Her feet were cold.

Knock-knock-knock.

Lacey suddenly remembered. Chester! Gina had left a note about coming over to help look for him!

Within seconds, she was up and out of bed. She grabbed the clothes she'd discarded in a heap by her bedside last night and hurriedly pulled them on. Then she was flying down the stairs, two at a time.

She ran to the back door, stooping down to grab her wellies off the shoe rack, while pulling the door open with her spare hand.

"Morning," Gina said, sounding as if the sight of Lacey contorted position amused her.

Lacey shoved a foot hastily into a wellie. "Thanks for the note. And the quiche."

Boudica bounded inside, nuzzling Lacey with excitement and almost causing her to lose her balance. She hopped around momentarily on one foot as she fought to stay upright. Then she steadied herself, and grappled with the other boot.

"Ready?" Gina asked.

Lacey grabbed her mac and Chester's leash from its hook.

"Ready," she said with a nod.

She swirled out into the brisk spring morning.

The pair of friends took the single track road that weaved through the cliffs, then strolled along the sidewalk toward town. Boudica kept her nose to the air, but there was no sign of Chester whatsoever.

When they reached the bottom of the high street, they realized that none of the cafes were open yet, and that they'd arrived before the breakfast shift. The only place open was the coffee shop to catch the early commuters, but Lacey was wary of the place after its owner had accused her of being a murderer. In fact, she'd not even set foot inside it after that day. But this was for Chester. She could swallow her pride for her beloved dog.

"I'm going in," Lacey said, with determination.

"You're brave," Gina told her.

"Brave? More like desperate."

Lacey pushed open the glass doors and entered the steamy cafe. Just her luck, it was the very lady at the counter who'd accused her. The woman did a double take when she saw who it was coming in.

"What do you want?" she asked, in a tone that suggested she was affronted.

Lacey held her hand up in truce position. "I just want to know if you've seen my dog, that's all. He's lost. I haven't seen him since yesterday."

The woman folded her arms and shot Lacey a withering look. "You mean, you've not seen him since you were arrested?"

Lacey felt her stomach tense. So the gossip had already spread. It had been less than twenty-four hours since she'd been hauled off in the police cruiser and *already* the town was whispering about her. Lacey felt tears welling in her eyes once again.

"Just let me know if you see him," she mumbled, before hurrying out.

Back in the streets, Lacey made a beeline for Gina.

Her friend looked up. "Any luck?"

Lacey shook her head, and took her arm for support. She didn't feel like telling Gina what had just transpired, so just said, "Let's keep going."

They headed down the high street, entering the stores that Lacey hoped would either not have heard the news about her arrest yet, or if they had, were kind enough not to give her the cold shoulder. Unfortunately, neither seemed to exist. Everyone had heard, and everyone was wary.

"This is just like last time," Lacey said, feeling glum. "Only worse. Because now I don't even have Chester for company."

It was at that moment that Lacey noticed a familiar face through the glass of one of the cafes.

"Tom?" she stammered, squinting to get a better look.

He was sat at a table nestled in the middle of the cafe, surrounded by other full tables, but he was not alone. There was another person with him. A woman. He was having breakfast with another woman.

Lacey staggered back as if the sight had physically pained her, and thudded into Gina's back.

"What is it?" her friend asked.

"Tom..." Lacey said, pointing at the window. "He's in there with another woman."

"Oh," Gina said simply, in a sad, sympathetic tone.

Lacey swirled on her heel and began marching down the high street. Boudica raced up beside her, and a moment later Gina appeared at her side as well, puffing and panting to keep up.

"Are you sure it wasn't Heidi?" Gina said, as she trotted alongside her.

"His mom? She's a strawberry blond! That woman was clearly a brunette."

She spoke between her teeth, beyond furious. Tom had seemed so distracted over the last few days, and she'd put it down to how busy his store was at the moment. Had it been because of another woman all along?

Lacey's own store came into view, and she felt the relief of knowing she'd soon be safe inside. But then she noticed the police car parked outside.

"What now?" Lacey exclaimed.

Her brisk stride turned it a jog as she hurried to find out what was going on. Poor Gina was left behind, neither fit enough nor stress-panicking enough to keep up.

When Lacey reached the car, she found DCI Beth Lewis leaning against its hood, a coffee cup in one hand. When she saw her, she uncrossed her legs. She'd evidently been waiting for Lacey's arrival.

"What's going on?" Lacey said through her panting breath. "Are you arresting me again?"

With an apologetic look on her face, DCI Lewis handed Lacey a slip of paper.

Lacey read it hurriedly, the letters dancing in front of her eyes with the trembling coming from her hands.

"I'm not allowed to open my store?" she exclaimed, looking up, aghast.

Beth shifted uncomfortably from one foot to the other. "I'm sorry, Lacey. Superintendent Turner wants forensics in there to see if they can collect DNA to link Xavier to the theft, and possibly the murder."

Lacey couldn't believe it. She was stunned. "What am I supposed to do?" she asked, lamely.

Beth shrugged. "Just take the day off? Have a bath or something."

Lacey fought the urge to shove her. What a stupid thing to say. It wasn't like she was on a salary and could just skip work for fun. This was her livelihood!

She paced away from the store, heading back to Gina, who'd given up trying to catch up with her and had slowed to the pace of a snail.

"What's going on, ducky?" her friend asked.

"My life is going down the toilet, that's what's going on," Lacey stammered. "Come on, let's go the beach route. We can check in with Brooke to see if Chester made it back to her tearoom."

They headed up the high street, beelining for the beach.

As they went, Lacey felt her phone begin to vibrate in her pocket. Hopeful that it might be the microchipping company calling about Chester, she grabbed it and checked the caller ID. It was David.

What does he want? Lacey thought with a mental groan.

She answered the call, because there really wasn't anything else the day could throw at her to make things worse. And maybe having a showdown with David would make her feel better?

"Yes?" she said hurriedly, the second she picked up the call.

"It's customary to answer the phone with hello," David said. "Or is that how they do it in England?"

Lacey paused. He didn't sound as aggressive as he had recently. In fact, it sounded like he was in good spirits.

"What do you want?" Lacey asked. "Because whatever it is, it needs to be quick. I have to keep this line open in case the microchip company calls to say they've found my missing dog."

"*You* have a dog?" David asked.

"Yes. But he's gone missing."

"I'm sorry. What's his name?"

"David!" Lacey yelled, losing her patience.

"—You called your dog David?" he joked.

"—Why are you calling?" Lacey snapped.

On the other end of the line, she heard his intake of breath.

"I wanted to let you know that things are over between me and Eda."

Lacey raised her eyebrows. "That was quick. What happened?"

"Nothing dramatic. We just realized we weren't right for each other."

"Ah. So the nineteen-year age gap came between you in the end?"

"Lace. Don't mock me. I'm calling because . . . because this time apart has made me realize a lot of things. And one of the things I've realized is that we had it really good before. And I was an idiot to throw all that away. I think you should come home and try and make a go of it with me. We can get your dog a doggy passport and bring him over."

Lacey listened to his monologue, a part of her brain genuinely considering it. Because what good had really come of her move to England? She'd gotten no closer to finding her father, and had ended up in a heap of trouble. She had the local police officers on speed dial, for goodness sake! She'd found a dog and lost him. Found a boyfriend and apparently lost him as well. And she was certain there was no way she'd be forgiven by the folks of Wilfordshire a second time. There was no way she wasn't losing her reputation this time.

All of those thoughts in Lacey's mind was the reason why she found herself saying, "I'll think about it."

"You will?" David said, and the glee in his voice was audible. "Your mother will be thrilled."

"I'm sure she will."

Lacey realized then that she and Gina had traveled all the way to the other end of the high street, where the ocean and promenade were visible. The sight of the sea prompted a sudden brainwave in Lacey.

"The island!" she exclaimed.

On the other end of the line, she heard David's voice saying, "Huh? Island? Or Ireland? What did you say?"

But Lacey wasn't listening to him anymore. She was staring at Gina and Boudica.

"The island!" she cried again.

Gina's eyes widened as it dawned on her what Lacey was trying to say.

"Of course!" she exclaimed, hopping from foot to foot. "Chester went to the island!"

Boudica, picking up on the sudden excitement from the human folk, started barking.

"Lacey?" came David's voice. "Lacey is everything okay? What's all that shouting and barking about? Are you being attacked? Do I need to call the cops?"

"I'm fine," she told him, hurriedly. "I've got to go."

She ended the call before he had a chance to say anything more, then together with Gina and Boudica, raced off toward the beach, feeling hopeful for the first time all day.

Chapter Eighteen

Lacey stood at the shoreline, staring out across the ocean. The tide was high, with no sign of the sandbar. Across the waves, she could just make out the island, the place she was absolutely certain Chester must be. There were no police trawlers moored there anymore, nor any police tape. Their investigations on the island must be over.

Of course it is, Lacey thought sadly, *because now they're focusing on my store. And Xavier.*

She still couldn't quite believe that Xavier might be responsible. He didn't seem the sort. But then again, who exactly did? Real murderers weren't like the ones in stories, with hunchbacks and limps and clammy, pockmarked faces. In the real world, murderers looked like normal people. Like Xavier.

She shuddered and forced her mind back to the problem at hand: getting to the island.

"How are we going to get across?" she asked Gina.

"The sandbar won't be out until the evening," Gina said. "We'll have to call Tom and ask him to bring down his boat."

"No way," Lacey said, as the memory of Tom having breakfast with the brunette flashed into her mind's eye. "I am *not* getting Tom to play my knight in shining armor. There must be someone else we can ask. Come on Gina. You must know someone who owns a boat."

Just then, Gina's eyebrows rose up her forehead. "There *is* someone we could call."

"Who?"

"The volunteer coast guards. I know all the lads from that time I got stuck on the island. Nice bunch of fellas."

"Would they help us? I thought they were there to rescue fishermen in distress. This isn't exactly an emergency."

"I don't know," Gina said. "They might tell us to hop it. But, on the other hand, they might fancy taking the boat out for a spin. It's not like they get much use out of it. If it's been a quiet week, they might fancy it. Here, hand me your phone. It's worth a shot."

She held her hand out, and Lacey placed her cell in it. She watched, nervously chewing on her fingernails, as Gina dialed a number and put the phone to her ear.

"Jacob!" she exclaimed into the speaker. "Long time no see. I was hoping to catch you."

She gave Lacey a wink and paced away, to continue her phone-flirting with Jacob the Volunteer Coast Guard in privacy.

While she was gone, Lacey strained to see whether she could catch a glimpse of Chester on the island. There was no sign of him. Even if he was there, he'd be too small to be seen from this distance. The trees and castle ruins were barely visible, so an English Shepherd certainly wouldn't be.

Just then, Gina returned to Lacey's side and handed her back her cell phone with a triumphant grin. "We're in luck. They said they'd help us. There's just one condition."

"What's that?" Lacey asked anxiously.

"I have to go on a date with Jake."

Lacey's eyes widened with surprise. "Oh. Is that a good thing? Or are you falling on your sword for me?"

Gina shrugged. "Well, it's been about a decade since I went on a date, so I'm not picky. But you can decide for yourself when he gets here."

"When are they coming?" Lacey asked.

"He said they'd leave right away," Gina told her. She pointed back along the shoreline, in the direction of Brooke's tearoom. "The lifeguard house is over there, next to the rowing school."

Of course, Lacey thought, remembering how Brooke's cafe was in a converted canoe shed. It stood to reason the maritime buildings were bunched up together. There were probably even more farther along the promenade. She'd have to explore some time.

"There it is!" Gina exclaimed.

Lacey squinted, and saw a small black dot on the horizon.

"Blimey, you have good eyesight," Lacey said.

Gina burst out laughing. "Since when did you say blimey?!"

Lacey blushed. "I guess I picked it up from you."

"I'll take that as a compliment," Gina said. "Now, how do I look?"

The lifeboat was coming toward them at quite a speed, bringing the lothario Jacob ever closer.

Lacey glanced from Gina's oversized yellow rain mac down to her olive green wellington boots.

"As beautiful as ever," she said.

The buzzing sound of the boat turned to a roar as it sped up in the waters ahead of them. Then one of the men aboard anchored it, while the other leapt down into the shallow waters and began striding toward them.

"Which one is Jacob?" Lacey asked, nudging Gina.

"The one walking toward us," Gina replied. "With the ginger beard."

The man was close enough for Lacey to see the missing teeth behind his grin.

"Oh Gina," Lacey said, squeezing her friend's arms. She truly had made a sacrifice.

Jacob reached them, sloshing water as he drew to a halt. "Good morning, ladies. I understand you require our services to rescue a dog."

His eloquent speech did *not* match his commoner's accent or rough fisherman appearance, and Lacey couldn't help but find the juxtaposition quite charming.

"You're our heroes!" Gina said, laying on the charm offensive rather thickly.

As Jacob helped her aboard, Gina batted her lashes. Lacey, though offered an arm by the other lifeguard—a skinny man who looked far too young to be anywhere but school—declined, choosing instead to clambered her own way on.

With them both inside the raft, Jacob handed them lifejacket. They were a lurid coral hue that would probably make Taryn weep. Then the engine buzzed to life and the boat began its short journey to the island.

"A missing dog, aye?" the man-boy said as they went. "There's a lot of silly things we've been called out for, but a missing dog is definitely a first." He smirked.

"I must warn you two ladies," Jacob said, "There's been some gruesome business around these parts recently. A murder, if you can believe it. On this very island."

Lacey felt the strangest swell of relief at his words, to know that there were *some* people in Wilfordshire who didn't instantly recognize her as the lady from the antique store who'd gotten arrested on suspicion of aiding and abetting a murderer. Maybe there was still hope for her yet.

It took barely two minutes to reach the island's jetty in the speedy rescue boat, and before Jacob and his less-eloquent companion had a chance to tie the boat up, Boudica had already leapt out and gone tearing off into the undergrowth, barking like a lunatic.

Lacey's chest lifted. "Is that a good sign?" she asked Gina.

Gina gave a cautious nod. "She's smelt something, that's for sure."

She and Lacey clambered over the edge of the boat.

"We'll wait here!" Jacob called as they trekked toward the trees. "Watch yourselves! There's a whistle and torch on your life jacket if you need any assistance!"

Gina flashed Jacob a thumbs up, then she and Lacey disappeared into the undergrowth after Boudica.

As they reached the center of the thicket, Lacey picked up the most blessed sound ever. Two distinct barks.

She grabbed Gina's arm. "It's him! It's Chester!"

They hurried on, making it out the other side of the trees. And there, galloping toward her, tail making circles as he ran, was Chester.

Lacey's vision blurred instantly as her eyes filled with tears. She crouched down, arms open to him. Chester leapt up and put his paws on her shoulders so forcefully she was knocked backwards. But she didn't care at all. She had her beloved dog back!

"Oh, Chester, you had me worried!" Lacey exclaimed, as she ruffled his fur and snuggled into him. "Never do that again, you naughty, awful, horrible, wonderful, beautiful, special boy. Okay!"

"Hey, Lacey," Gina said.

Lacey stopped her wrestle with Chester and looked over at her friend. "What?"

"Look at this. Chester dropped it out of his mouth when he came running for you."

Lacey heaved herself up to her feet and headed toward Gina. Chester, clearly working out what they were looking at, pelted over and snapped up whatever it was in his jaws.

"Give it here," Lacey told him, holding out her hand.

He dropped it at her feet.

What on earth... Lacey thought, as she picked the object up and inspected it in her hands. It appeared to be the strap of a leather handbag, torn, as if it had been ripped violently off. It was a very familiar-looking handbag, Lacey thought, perhaps one that Taryn stocked. Then she realized the color was dusky pink. Last season's dusky pink. The same color as the dresses Daisy had bought from Taryn's boutique. The same color as the bag...

Lacey squeaked and dropped the handle. She staggered back, staring at the dusky pink leather strap. If that was indeed the handle of Daisy's bag, then its presence here on the island was evidence that she'd been here too! It corroborated Xavier's sighting!

"What is it?" Gina asked, sounding concerned.

Lacey glanced from the torn handle lying in the sand by her feet, over to her friend. "I think I might have just found something that makes Daisy's alibi fall apart."

Chapter Nineteen

Lacey was so relieved to have Chester back. But as she huddled beside him on the coast guard's boat, cutting through the waves back to shore, her mind was troubled. The leather strap was in the pocket of her rain mac but Lacey knew that once she made it back to shore, she'd have to work out what to do with it.

Of course, any sane person would hand it over to the police. In fact, any sane person probably would've called them immediately rather than picking it up and putting it in their pocket. But Lacey had literally only just gotten out of their interrogation room and the last thing she wanted to do was walk right back in there. But she also knew she may very well be in possession of a crucial piece of evidence. One that may expose Daisy's alibi as a fake. That might help get Xavier free.

They reached shore, and Lacey climbed out the boat with her mind in a jumble. Behind her, Jacob helped Gina out.

"I look forward to our future meeting," he said, in his odd way. Then to Lacey, he added, "I'm delighted your pet has been reunited with you. For now, we shall bid you adieu."

"See ya," the skinny man added.

As the volunteer boat buzzed away, Gina looked over at Lacey.

"Penny for your thoughts? You've been ever so quiet. I thought you'd be over the moon to have Chester back."

Lacey looked over at her canine companion, now frolicking with Boudica without a care in the world, as if he hadn't just spent the entire night stuck on an abandoned island worrying everyone half to death.

"I'm thrilled, of course," she said. "I'm just . . . I guess I'm exhausted. Things have been pretty stressful. I can't remember the last time I had a proper sleep."

Gina rubbed her shoulder. "Why don't you head home? Take a nap. It's not like you can open the store today."

"Don't remind me," Lacey said with a groan, remembering the official *police notice to commandeer property* folded up in her pocket that DCI Lewis had handed her.

"Go home," Gina urged her. "You look haggard, girl. And I'm sure Chester could do with a rest as well. I'm heading into town. I'll let Tom know Chester's back."

"Alright, thank you," Lacey said, glad that she had a friend to look for her well-being.

She said goodbye to Gina and climbed the cliff path up to her back garden, Chester at her heels. Once she made it inside her house, the tiredness she'd been feeling seemed to multiply. Now her limbs felt heavy, like they were made of steel. Lacey was just about ready to pass out.

She peeled off her clothes as she trudged up the staircase, discarding each piece on the steps as she went, much to Chester's bemusement—he started barking, then took her socks in his mouth as if trying to work out whether this was a new game of fetch. Then she reached her room and flopped, face first, into bed.

It was too bright to sleep, so Lacey pulled the curtains shut. They were pretty good at blocking out most of the daylight, but she still couldn't relax. There was too much on her mind. She'd barely had time to process that Tom had been having breakfast with another woman. And that David had asked to try again. And that she may be in possession of a piece of evidence that could nail a killer and exonerate an innocent man!

It was all too much.

With her mind swirling, Lacey decided to try an eye pillow. It was something she'd often had to resort to while living in New York City, particularly on loud days like public holidays. But it was still no use.

She sat up. At the foot of her bed, the lump that was Chester was snoring soundly.

"Good for you," Lacey said, patting his head. "But I think I'm going to have to resort to slightly more extreme measures."

She took the packet of sleeping pills out of her bedside dresser and popped a couple. Then she lay back and waited for them to kick in.

Which was of course the perfect time for her phone to ding with the sound of an incoming email. Lacey hesitated. It might not be a good idea to check her mail moments before she drifted off into a drug induced sleep. She might influence her dreams. But she also couldn't quite resist. Knowing there was an unread notification on her phone was like having an itch that demanded to be scratched. She took it off her dresser and opened the email app.

The message was from her bank. A reminder about the bank holiday at the end of May, and how it might affect scheduled payments. Realizing it would delay David's alimony once again, Lacey logged into her mobile banking app to make a one off adjustment.

As she did, she couldn't help noticing the transactions of the last few days, particularly since one had a bright red exclamation point beside it. It appeared to be from the day of the auction, and the transaction it was related to was in dollars.

"Buck's," Lacey said, with a small gasp. "That's his payment for the sextant." She tapped on the notification.

Payment suspended. This is due to suspicious and potentially fraudulent activity on the payer's account, and is in no way the fault of British Building and Bank.

"Huh," Lacey said.

She could understand why Buck's accounts would be paused after his death, but the notice specifically mentioned suspicious activity. Although it could've just been a generic notification that got attached to all payments that were suspended by the other side. Either way, the important thing was that she hadn't been paid for the sextant. She'd almost guessed it wouldn't happen. It was the icing on the cake really. The rare item was in police custody, evidence in a murder trial, and she hadn't received any recompense for it. Now, she probably never would.

She yawned, the pills finally starting to kick in.

"I wonder if Buck was having financial troubles," Lacey thought, before she conked out and fell into a deep, deep sleep.

CHAPTER TWENTY

Lacey awoke feeling groggy. She'd forgotten how sleeping pills could do that to her. They could also make her feel very vacant and forgetful.

When she checked the time, she realized she'd been asleep for about five hours. It was now evening.

Chester sat up at her movements.

"Do you want some dinner?" she asked him.

He barked.

"I thought as much," Lacey said.

As she went downstairs, she passed her discarded clothes on the steps, and suddenly remembered the pink leather bag strap that was still in her coat pocket.

"Last season's dusky pink . . ." she said aloud.

Her senses seemed to be slowly coming back to her, as she reached into the kitchen cabinet and retrieved the bag of doggy kibble. As she began pouring it into Chester's bowl, she suddenly exclaimed, "Brooke!" Her friend always gave Chester kibble when they visited the tearoom. "I didn't call her to tell her you were back home safe. She was so worried!"

Guilty about the amount of time that had lapsed, Lacey grabbed the kitchen phone and punched in Brooke's number. She paced back and forth across the tiles as she listened to the ring tone. The cord stretched like an elastic band as she zigzagged around the room.

Finally, the phone was answered. "Wilfordshire Tearoom. Brooke speaking. How can I help?"

"Brooke. It's Lacey."

"Lacey! Are you okay?" She sounded frantic with worry. "I went past your store earlier and saw the police had locked it up! What's going on?"

"They're doing forensics tests," Lacey explained. "Searching for DNA. But that's not why I'm calling. I wanted to let you know that Chester's back home."

"He is?" Brooke gushed. "What a relief. Where was he?"

"I found him on the island. He must have run across the sandbar and gotten stuck when the tide rose."

"The ... island?" Brooke asked, sounding like she couldn't quite believe it.

"Yeah. He's totally obsessed with the place. I think he's trying to solve the murder. He even found some evidence while he was over there. Something the police missed."

There was a moment of silence on the line.

"What did he find?" Brooke said finally.

"The strap of a bag. Looks like it was torn off, probably during the struggle. But here's the interesting thing. It's from a bag Taryn sold in her boutique. I know it because it's in last season's dusky pink. Taryn must've sold it to the murderer. To someone who didn't care it was about to go out of season. To someone who only cared about the color." She paused, waiting for Brooke to fill in the blank. But when she was met by yet more silence, she prompted her friend, "The *pink* color."

"I've not been here long enough to know everyone in Wilfordshire's favorite colors," the Aussie replied, wryly.

"Daisy!" Lacey exclaimed. "She wears something pink with every outfit. And they'd arrived in Wilfordshire just before Taryn swapped her stock."

"Wow, that's some impressive detective work," Brooke exclaimed. "What are you going to do? Give the strap to the police?"

"Not yet," Lacey confessed. "I'm not in a rush to see them so soon, you know?"

Brooke let out a sad laugh. "I am truly sorry about what happened yesterday. I was so convinced the Spanish man had done it. I thought you'd lost your marbles sitting there talking to him like that! But I didn't think the police would arrest you as well."

"It's okay," Lacey told her. "You couldn't have known. Besides, if I hadn't been arrested, Chester would never have run off, and the strap would never have been found. Everything happens for a reason." Her voice trailed off as she suddenly remembered Buck's failed wire transfer last night. "Hey, Brooke. Did Buck and Daisy pay for their breakfast that time they came to yours?"

"Yes ..." her friend replied, drawing out the word with confusion. "Why do you ask?"

"Because I'm trying to work out Daisy's motive," Lacey replied. "I think it might be related to money. How did they pay? Cash or card?"

"Card."

"Can you check your online bank account for me? Because my payment from them was suspended due to suspicious and potentially fraudulent activity."

"Sure," Brooke replied, though she didn't sound too thrilled.

Lacey waited, listening to the sound of Brooke tapping onto a keyboard.

"What d'ya know!" the Aussie exclaimed a second later. "I have the same message. Fraudulent activity. What are you thinking?"

"I'm thinking Buck didn't actually have the funds to pay for any of the stuff he bought Daisy in Wilfordshire. Either he used to be wealthy but lost it somehow, or he was just pretending to impress her, but my hunch is it all came to a head during their vacation and Daisy found out."

"Do you reckon she killed him for the insurance?" Brooke asked. "It wouldn't be the first time a young wife killed an older lover for money."

She sounded a little too keen, like Carla in the B'n'B, but without the excuse of youth to justify it.

"I'm not so sure about that," Lacey said. "It seems too calculating for Daisy."

"Ooh!" Brooke said, her excitement ratcheting up even more. "I bet she got him to row her over to the island where there'd be no witnesses, then went berserk-o and killed him!"

Despite how distasteful Lacey felt Brooke was being, she did consider her theory momentarily. But it didn't quite fit. It seemed too cold for Daisy to have premeditated the murder, not to mention the fact she didn't seem smart enough to come up with a plan like that. And what about the fact Buck was double her size? If she'd planned to kill him, surely she would have brought a weapon.

"No, it was opportunistic," Lacey explained. "A spur of the moment thing. I think Daisy found out about Buck's debts and challenged him. Well, we both know how easily Buck's pride gets damaged when it comes to money. I think he retaliated physically. Raised his fist. Daisy ran. He got hold of her bag by the handle, yanking it back. But the strap tore, and he fell. A big, unhealthy guy like Buck isn't going to be able to get up very fast, and Daisy, fearing for her life, jumped on his back and pushed him down into the sand until he stopped moving."

The whole scenario played out in her mind's eye. After realizing she'd killed her husband, Daisy rowed back to shore, distraught, where Xavier witnessed her alone and crying. Then she must have pulled herself together and headed to Taryn's, knowing she'd be captured on the CCTV cameras, providing an alibi, as long as the police didn't check the clocks too stringently. She either held Taryn up at the store for so long because she wanted as much footage of her as possible, or because she was so freaked out about what had happened she didn't want to be alone. If Taryn was selling her last season's stock, perhaps she took her into the back room, with a view over the gardens. Daisy might have seen Gina watering the plants under the moonlight, and leaving the back door unlocked. That would've given her the idea to plant the sextant and frame Lacey.

It all fit perfectly! The puzzle had come together, with every piece of evidence Lacey had gathered accounted for, and everything she knew of Buck's and Daisy's personalities and financial situation filling in the blanks. For the first time since she'd stumbled upon Buck's pale, lifeless body, Lacey saw the light at the end of the tunnel. She'd cracked it. It was almost over. She just had to prove it . . .

Lacey suddenly realized that the other end of the line was silent. It had been silent for so long, she wondered whether the call had disconnected.

"Brooke?" she asked. "You there?"

When Brooke finally replied, her voice was filled with emotion. "Sorry. The way you described it . . . it reminded me of my ex-hubby."

Lacey gasped. How could she have been so insensitive! Brooke had told her all about her violent ex, and she'd just put her foot right in.

"I'm so sorry, Brooke. Are you okay?"

The woman sniffed. But then her tone suddenly changed. "You'll never guess who just walked in."

"Who?" Lacey asked.

Brooke replied in a stunned whisper. "Daisy!"

Lacey was immediately alert. This was it. Her chance. If she could put the pressure on Daisy with the evidence and theory, then she could get the woman to confess.

She squeezed the receiver tightly, as adrenaline began to course through her.

"Listen, I need you to stall her. Do everything you can to keep her in your tearoom. Lock her in if you have to. I'll be there as soon as possible."

She put down the phone and looked at Chester. He quirked his head to the side, flashing her his perceptive expression.

"It's time to nail this killer once and for all," she said. "You ready?"

Chester barked.

CHAPTER TWENTY ONE

"This had better be good," Superintendent Turner said as Lacey strolled up to him.

He was standing with his ass leaned against his car, parked up on the sea-front outside Brooke's tearoom. She was surprised he'd made it there before her, since she'd driven twice the speed limit to get here.

"Oh, it's good," Lacey said confidently. "Like I said on the phone, I've solved your murder."

The detective raised an eyebrow. "I highly doubt that."

But Lacey felt very certain of herself, and by the way Chester was walking by her side with his chin up and chest puffed out, made her feel that he supported her as well.

She gestured to the automatic glass doors as they swished open. "Gentlemen first."

Superintendent Turner gave her his dead-eyed look and didn't move.

"Fine," Lacey said. "I'll lead the way."

She went in through the automatic doors.

True to her word, Brooke had managed to keep Daisy inside the tearoom. The young widow was clad in her signature pink, and was seated in one of the half-boat booths. By the looks of the various empty dishes around her, Brooke had been plying her with cakes.

Brooke herself was anxiously chewing on her nails. When she saw Lacey entering, she hurried over.

"You took your time," she whispered frantically. "I'm pretty sure Daisy thinks I'm attempting to date her with all that free cake!" But her expression suddenly changed as her gaze went past Lacey to Superintendent Turner. "You brought the fuzz with you?"

"Someone has to arrest her once I've forced her to confess," Lacey whispered back.

Brooke looked uncomfortable, and Lacey squeezed her friend's arm.

"Relax. You did your bit. I'll take it from here."

"Lacey," Superintendent Turner snapped. He threw his arm toward Daisy sitting alone in the booth. "What the hell is going on?"

Lacey gulped. "Just . . . let me do the talking."

The detective shook his head as if he'd just realized he'd made a terrible mistake coming here, but he followed Lacey as she walked over to the half-sawn rowing-boat nook Daisy was occupying.

At the sound of their footsteps, Daisy's head darted up. Her fork clattered to her plate. She couldn't have looked more guilty if she'd tried.

"What's going on?" she asked, her voice trembling. Clearly realizing she was about to be ambushed, she went to stand.

"Please, stay seated," Lacey said, gesturing for her to sit back down.

Daisy sank into the cushions like a popped balloon.

Superintendent Turner looked more nonplussed than ever. "I'm not sitting in that thing."

"Sit," Lacey told him, firmly.

He sighed, and did, perching right on the edge.

Lacey squeezed into the uncomfortable seat beside him.

"What's going on?" Daisy asked again, looking even more guilty.

Lacey reached into her pocket and retrieved the leather bag handle. She thunked it triumphantly down onto the table.

Silence followed.

"What's that?" Superintendent Turner said.

But Lacey kept her focus intently on Daisy. She was expecting to see the woman squirm. For there to be some reaction from her. But she was keeping her poker face.

"You recognize it, don't you, Daisy?" Lacey said.

"Yes," Daisy replied.

Ha! Lacey thought. *I've got you cornered now.*

"Do you want to tell Superintendent Turner what it is, or shall I?"

Daisy looked bemused. "I don't know why he'd want to know."

Karl Turner was starting to look thoroughly frustrated. He turned to Lacey. "Tell me what it is now or I'll book you for wasting police time."

"Fine," Lacey said, casting a cold glance at Daisy. "*That* is a piece of evidence from the island that your officers failed to find. Chester retrieved it last night."

She felt triumphant. But Superintendent Turner didn't react with gratitude at all. In fact, he was almost out of his seat with shock.

"This was on the island?" he exclaimed. "And you touched it? Without gloves?" He reached into his pocket and pulled out a glove and baggie, then got to work bagging up the strap, huffing as he did.

"I don't carry gloves and evidence bags around as habit," Lacey replied tersely. "I mean, I know I do an awful lot of your job for you, but believe it or not, I'm not actually a police officer."

She'd been expecting some gratitude, not accusations, and felt put out.

"If that *is* evidence," Superintendent Turner said, his face turning red, "you've completely invalidated it by getting your dirty hands and slobbery dog all over it!"

But Lacey's lack of gloves was hardly the matter here. At least it wouldn't be once she'd gotten a confession out of Daisy.

"What even is it?" the detective finished, inspecting the item that was now successfully bagged.

Lacey looked at Daisy again. She was playing it cool. Very cool. Probably thanks to Superintendent Turner blurting out that the evidence was useless. Lacey would have to put the pressure on if she wanted to get her to confess.

"It's the handle of a bag," she explained. "A bag stocked in Taryn's boutique. A bag in last season's dusky pink. Daisy's favorite color."

Superintendent Turner looked at Lacey, aghast. He started shaking his head. "Don't. No. Don't tell me you dragged me out here because you think Daisy . . ." He stopped speaking and huffed loudly.

"You think I'm what?" Daisy asked, looking perturbed.

Superintendent Turner looked like he was about to explode with rage. "She thinks you're a killer," he said, scathingly. "Because of your fashion choices! Even though there's CCTV footage that corroborates your alibi."

Daisy's bottom lip started to quiver. "You think I killed Bucky . . . ?"

Lacey frowned at the detective. "The clock on the machine must be wrong. Either that, or the time of death is incorrect."

Daisy burst into tears.

Superintendent Turner didn't seem to notice though. He was focusing all his attention, anger and fury at Lacey.

"You're so big-headed that you'll assume a computerized machine and a skilled mortician are more likely to be wrong than you? This is unbelievable!"

A sudden *thunk* made Lacey and Karl jump. Daisy had slammed her bag onto the table in front of them. Just as Lacey had expected, it was the dusky pink one.

For a second, Lacey thought the woman was about to confess. But then she realized Daisy had a very different reason for slamming her bag in front of them like that. She was showing off the handles. The two very intact handles.

A sudden, awful dawning came over Lacey. Had she got it wrong? But... everything fit! Didn't it?

"I didn't kill my husband," Daisy squeaked. "I loved him, even if he was a crook."

Lacey and Superintendent Turner exchanged a glance.

"Oh come on, you all know it!" Daisy exclaimed passionately. "He was a fraud. His first car lot went bust after Christmas. He said it was fine, the other three would soak up the trade and we'd be back on our feet in no time. But then the second lot went bust. Then the third. It seemed like the more they failed, the more he spent, as if he had to prove a point. I tried everything to get him to stop. If I'm guilty of anything, it's not knowing how to help." She looked up, and mascara streaked from her eyes as her tears fell. "I thought if I kept pushing him to spend on more and more stupid stuff, eventually he'd reach his breaking point. I mean, I even dragged him to your auction because I thought he might just see that the last thing we needed to buy was an antique frickin' boat thing!"

As she listened to Daisy's desperate story, humiliation started to build in Lacey's guts. She'd gotten it so, so wrong.

"But why did you look so guilty when you saw us?" Lacey said.

"Because I just ate about 2,000 calories worth of cake!" Daisy wailed. "And I'm not even supposed to eat gluten! But now Buck's gone, I just don't care anymore..."

She broke down, her head flopping into her arms across the table.

Lacey didn't want to look at Superintendent Turner. She side-eyed him. He was tight-jawed, glaring at her.

Without saying a word, he stood and paced away.

Lacey flew to her feet and hurried after him.

"I'm sorry," she said, reaching for his arm and stopping him in his tracks.

He swirled to face her with a thunderous expression. "Sorry isn't going to cut it when the widow of a murdered man sues the police department for accusing her of murder on little more than a pink bloody bag strap!"

He stormed out of the cafe.

Lacey watched him go, her chest heavy with humiliation.

She was back at square one.

CHAPTER TWENTY TWO

Brooke placed the cappuccino down in front of Lacey and took the bench opposite.

"I'm sorry your theory didn't play out," she said. "That whole altercation looked super uncomfortable."

"It was embarrassing," Lacey said, glancing over at the vacant nook Daisy had previously occupied. She turned back and smooshed the coffee froth art with her spoon. "I was so certain I'd cracked it."

"If it's any consolation, I thought you had as well," Brooke replied.

Lacey took a sip. The coffee was divine. Brooke really did make the best coffee in Wilfordshire.

She placed the cup back on the saucer. "I just keep thinking, if the strap wasn't from Daisy's bag, then whose was it from?"

Brooke drummed her fingers on the table, obviously trying to think it through as well. "This might sound a bit out there, but is there a chance it *was* from her bag, but she had the handle fixed to cover up the fact it was torn?"

"That's a good idea," Lacey said, pondering it. "But I wonder if that would've even been possible, given the time frame. It's not like a boutique item can be fixed by the local cobbler."

"Well then that could be why she went to Taryn's in the first place?" Brooke suggested. "To swap it with one that wasn't broken?"

It was an interesting theory, and Lacey mulled it over. It might explain why Daisy kept Taryn in the store so late, if she was trying to find an opportunity to swap the bags when the clerk wasn't looking.

"Thing is," Lacey said, "the bag is from last season's stock. Taryn said she specifically had to fetch last season's stuff because it was the only things she owned in pink. So the bag wouldn't have been on general sale anymore,

157

and Daisy would have had to ask her if she wanted a replacement. Taryn would have mentioned if Daisy had come back asking to buy *another* out of season handbag, I'm certain. Any reason to gossip." Lacey paused, as a sudden thought hit her. "Although . . . the handbag wasn't one of a kind. Taryn must've sold the same model to loads of different locals during the spring season. Maybe we could find out *who* bought one, and narrow down the suspect pool."

She looked at Brooke, expecting her friend's usual eager enthusiasm. But instead, Brooke's lips were twisted to the side. She looked uncomfortable. Troubled even.

"What's wrong?" Lacey asked.

Brooke hunched her shoulders. "I just worked out who did it."

"What? Who?" Lacey asked, her eyes widening.

Brooke looked even more uncomfortable, like she really didn't want to say it aloud. "Taryn."

Lacey's first instinct was to laugh, assuming Brooke was joking. But she could tell by the look on Brooke' face she was dead serious.

"Taryn?" Lacey repeated. "But she's . . ."

She stopped speaking. Was Brooke actually on to something? Taryn *was* a jilted business owner who'd been left out of pocket by Daisy's expensive purchases. She had a proven mean streak that bordered on psychotic, like the time she'd gotten her ex-convict handyman to prowl Lacey's cottage at night. Heck, maybe she'd gotten him involved in this as well? Hired him as a hit man to bump off Buck? Unlike Daisy, who didn't seem smart enough to plan a murder, Taryn was conniving to the bone. She may well have witnessed Gina's late night garden watering sessions and scattiness over locking the door, and come up with the plan to plant the sextant in the antiques store and frame Lacey.

But what about her state-of-the-art security system? It was Daisy's alibi, and that made it Taryn's alibi as well. Unless . . . Of course! As the owner of the system, Taryn had administrative powers to alter the clock!

Lacey gasped aloud as she realized Taryn fit neatly into the middle section of her Venn diagram.

"Daisy wasn't using Taryn as an alibi . . ." Lacey exclaimed. "Taryn was using Daisy!"

She was on her feet now, filled with adrenaline. Chester jumped up at her sudden excitement.

"Where are you going?" Brooke asked, looking perplexed.

"To follow up this lead," Lacey told her, excitedly. "Who knows, maybe I'll catch a killer by the end of the day, after all."

And with that, she hurried away, leaving Brooke blinking in her wake.

CHAPTER TWENTY THREE

The weather had turned since Lacey had first entered the tearoom. It was starting to get quite cloudy, and she could feel humidity building in the air. Her hair would be a ball of frizz before long, not that the condition of her hair mattered all that much; there were far more important things to deal with now.

She marched along the high street, which was darker than usual, since most of the stores had closed. The camp shop was still open, a tent pitched up outside to market how great their equipment was in the typical English spring drizzle. Lacey strolled past, feeling a bit sorry for the poor store clerk who had the unenviable job of sitting on a waterproof chair under waterproof awnings in a waterproof hat, jacket, pants and boots. The sandwich board beside him read: *It's May! May as well assume it's going to rain!*

As she went, Lacey looked down at Chester. He was walking obediently beside her with his chin held high, looking very purposeful.

She wondered if she'd been a bit hasty about Taryn. Her conversation with Brooke had been a tad frenzied, coming right off the back of the disaster with Daisy. But Brooke had thrown up some really interesting points with regards to Taryn's motives, and Lacey had filled in the blanks regarding motive fairly swiftly. Yes, it had been rushed, but at the same time, Lacey wasn't prepared to leave any stone unturned, especially if it meant another night in jail for an innocent man.

The rain was falling when she reached the boutique. The glaring lights coming through its windows seeming suddenly very unpleasant, illuminating off the quickly forming puddles.

"The sign was right," Lacey said to Chester. "May as well assume it's going to rain!"

She pushed open the door and went inside.

At the sound of her entrance, Taryn looked up from the counter. The second she registered who was entering her store, she started shaking her head.

"Nope! No, no, no. Get that dirty dog out of my store!"

She started walking toward Lacey, making shooing gestures.

But it was too late. Chester shook himself, and droplets of rainwater sprayed off his fur, glistening under the lights as they covered everything within a meter radius in a fine mist.

"Ah!" Taryn screeched. "That smell permeates! It gets into the clothes!" She grabbed the closest silky number. "Yes. I can smell it. This will have to be dry cleaned. I'll bill you. And I'll have to put a million tons of potpourri in the glass bowls now. I'll bill you for that as well."

Lacey listened to Taryn's monologue, squinting at the woman. She just didn't strike her as a killer. Anyone who got that flapped by a wet dog surely couldn't be capable of killing another human? The grossness alone would make her faint, wouldn't it?

Lacey inched back to the door, gesturing Chester outside, but keeping it open so he was still within range. She wasn't quite ready to let him stray too far, and having a glass door barrier between them was too much.

"Now what are you doing?" Taryn exclaimed. "You're letting all the heat out! Either get in or get out. No, actually, I'll make it easy. Just get out!"

"I have one question," Lacey said from her odd position, half in and half out the store. "Did you sell many of those pink bags last season?"

Taryn looked exasperated. "Why are you asking me that?"

Lacey hesitated. When she'd been speaking to Brooke earlier, it had seemed to make so much sense for Taryn to be involved in Buck's murder. But now that she was here, actually face to face with the woman, something in her mind told her it just wasn't possible.

"I found a piece of evidence," she said, treading cautiously nonetheless. "It links Buck's murder to your store."

"*My* store?" Taryn squeaked. Her face paled. "Oh god, are the cops going to come for me like they did you? I'll never live it down." She started flapping her hands with panic.

"Taryn. Calm Down," Lacey said. "Listen to me."

Taryn stopped and dropped her arms. The possibility of impending arrest had turned her to putty in Lacey's hands.

"Do you have a list of people you sold that model of bag to?" Lacey asked.

"A list?" Taryn exclaimed. "Of course I don't have a list! Do you keep a list of everyone you sell to?"

"Alright, alright. Not a list. But do you happen to remember?"

"No, I don't," Taryn said all in one breath. "They didn't sell that well at first, until I priced them down for the end of season sale. Then they flew off the shelves. Brenda bought one. Carol. Jane bought two—one for her and one for her sister-in-law . . ."

Brenda. Carol. Two people who had interactions with Buck.

"Melissa from the pie shop. Juliette the dog walker. Oh, and the florist, whose name I can't remember. I mean even Bu—"

"Don't worry," Lacey said, interrupting her with the shake of her head. "The bag was popular. A ton of people bought it. It won't narrow down my suspect list at all."

"Your suspect list?" Taryn wailed. She was starting to panic again.

All of a sudden, Lacey had an a-ha moment.

"Taryn. Listen. I need you to do something for me."

Once again, the boutique owner gave Lacey her full attention. "What now?" she said, sounding like a child on the verge of a meltdown.

"Don't worry, it'll be easy for you. It's something you do best. I need you to spread some gossip. Spread the word that I've worked out who the killer is. That I've found a big piece of evidence on the island, and am heading there now to fetch it. Say that once I've collected the piece of evidence, I'm going to expose the killer. Start at the Coach House. It'll spread like wildfire. I mean, the last rumor you started from there did."

Taryn pouted. "I already apologized for that."

Apologized was quite a loose term for what Taryn had done.

"Sure you did."

Lacey couldn't quite believe she was conspiring with her nemesis. But her instincts were telling her that Taryn wasn't the perp. This prim fashionista would never get her hands dirty. Besides, her hair was dark brown like Lacey's, and Xavier was sure the woman in the rowboat was blond. But once the news had spread around town, Lacey was certain that the real killer would come to the island in an attempt to find the piece of evidence before her, exposing themselves in the process.

Lacey checked the clock. The sandbar wouldn't be out for much longer. She'd have to hurry.

"I'd better go. Taryn, work your magic."

She raced out the boutique and along the high street. Now, the rain was starting to lash down. Heading to an abandoned island to catch a killer in wet weather wasn't really top of things Lacey wanted to do.

She saw the camping store ahead and rushed up to the clerk.

"I need some kind of tent. That's rainproof. And easy to assemble. I'm from New York."

The clerk laughed. "You'll want a pop-up then. We have the X45 model, or the X45a model which has an extra five inches of—"

"Either. I don't mind. Whichever gets you more commission."

The clerk looked thrilled. "In that case, maybe you'd be interested in the Orion model?"

Lacey shook her head. "Can we hurry up? I'm in a rush. I've got to beat the tide to get to the island."

The clerk gave her an uncertain expression. "I don't know if today's the best day to go camping. You've heard about the stor—"

But once again, Lacey cut him off. "Please. Can we hurry?"

He held his hands up. "Alright. Alright. I'll drop the sales pitch." He collected a pop-up tent from inside, and came back outside to meet her. "So what is it you're so desperate to get to the island for?"

"I found some evidence," Lacey said. "In the murder case of Buckland Stringer. I'm going over there to collect it from the island. It'll totally nail the murderer."

At long last, the clerk fell silent. Lacey had managed to wipe the chatter right off his face.

CHAPTER TWENTY FOUR

The drizzle had turned to fat, splotchy rain drops by the time Lacey and Chester reached the beach.

There was the smallest sliver of sandbar left.

Chester went right for it. Lacey, the slower of the two, brought up the rear. They'd just made it to the other side when the tide rose and cut them off.

"That was close," she said.

She looked down at the tent tucked under her arm. Pop-up. She unzipped it from its casing and watched as it popped, literally, into tent position. She hadn't thought about its color when she'd bought it, and was relieved to find it was khaki green. It would blend in nicely with the foliage.

She moved the tent to the trees, just as the rain turned to a deluge.

"Chester, quick, get inside," she told the dog.

She leapt in and he huddled in beside her.

Lacey peered out the flap, gazing at the ocean. There was no sign of the sandbar anymore, which meant there was no way off the island for her now, which was a slightly worrying thought. But at least the sound of the rain on the tent was relaxing.

Maybe I am cut out for this camping thing after all, Lacey thought.

Just then, she heard something. Chester heard it too; his ears pricked up. It was the sound of rowing.

Quietly, carefully, Lacey peered out.

The rain had created a gray haze over everything, making it difficult to see. Lacey squinted, and could just make out a small wooden rowboat coming toward her. But all she could see of the figure inside was their black silhouette.

Lacey shuddered, thinking about how she might have put herself in harm's way. But she couldn't tear her eyes away from the rowing boat as it inched closer and closer to land.

Then it tapped against the jetty.

Under the moonlight, Lacey watched the figure clamber out.

A woman, just like Xavier had witnessed. A blond woman.

Daisy? Lacey thought.

But as the figure came closer, she realized it wasn't Daisy at all. It was Brooke.

Confused, Lacey unzipped the flap of the tent and hurried out into the rain.

"Brooke?" she called over the sound of raindrops on leaves. "What are you doing here?"

"What am *I* doing here?" Brooke yelled back. "What are *you* doing? There's a storm coming! A bad one! I saw you running across the sandbar with Chester and jumped in my boat right away. You shouldn't be out here."

Lacey shook her head. "I need to be here. I need to do something."

Brooke raised an eyebrow, giving Lacey a look like she was mad, which, in fairness, Lacey sort of was right now.

"What?" Brooke cried over the rain. "What could you possibly need to do?"

If her friend thought she was mad merely for being on the island in a storm, what would she think if she found out Lacey was here to catch the local murderer? She decided to keep quiet.

"It's a wilderness thing," Lacey said, evasively. "Little bit spiritual. Little bit rugged survival skills."

The rain began to lash down.

"Let's get inside the tent," Lacey cried.

The two friends bundled inside. Lacey had only been in the rain for a matter of minutes, but she was already soaked to the bone. She zipped up the tent to keep out the driving rain.

"I can't believe you rowed all the way over here to fetch me," Lacey said to Brooke. "You're soaked. And I don't have a towel or anything."

"You seem pretty underprepared for the 'wilderness,'" Brooke joked, putting the last word in air quotes. "Are you sure you don't want me to row us both back to shore?."

Lacey shook her head again. "No. I need to stay. But you go. Don't feel like you have to stay for my sake. You know, I never guessed you'd be a rower."

"I'm a woman of many talents," Brooke replied. "Wrestler. Rower."

"What can't you do?" Lacey joked, using humor in an attempt to manage the stress of the situation. She leaned over and patted Chester's head. "When did you buy your boat, then? Considering you've only lived in Wilfordshire for a few weeks!"

"It was literally the day I moved here," Brooke explained. "I used to live by a lake. I'd fish there, and swim there. And whenever my ex smacked me around, I'd take the boat out right to the middle of the lake where it was quiet and calm. To get away from it all."

Her voice had become detached. The bubbly Aussie Lacey had gotten to know seemed suddenly distant. She recognized it as the same air of melancholy that had overcome her on the day of the auction, after her spat with Buck.

"I'm not surprised you felt the need to buy one when you moved here," Lacey said, gently.

Brooke nodded in affirmation. "It's like a security blanket. Whenever I feel threatened, I'll go for a row."

Lacey felt bad for the woman. "I'm really sorry you went through so much. I guess you came here for a quiet life, then got all this."

"All this?" Brooke asked.

"Buck and Daisy causing havoc. Buck's murder. It's been a pretty eventful time since you arrived."

Brooke seemed utterly dejected. She hitched her knees up to her chest and sighed wearily.

As she did, she exposed a backpack she'd brought with her, wedged into the corner of the tent. It looked strangely empty, as if there was next to nothing inside.

"What's in there?" Lacey asked, curiously.

Brooke looked over shoulder at the bag. She turned back and shrugged. "Nothing in particular. It's just my bag." Her tone had become slightly defensive.

Chester seemed to notice as well. His ears twitched, as if he was becoming more alert.

"So?" Brooke said. "I heard this weird rumor in the pub. That you'd found some evidence out here? Is it something other than the bag strap?"

For some reason, her question made Lacey feel uneasy. And with her uneasiness came a horrible sudden thought...was there a blank space on the Venn diagram for Brooke?

She quickly thought it through. For starters, Brooke was blond. Though she and Daisy had different hairstyles, in the darkness, it was the bright color of their hair that was most noticeable. Indeed, she and thought Brooke was Daisy when she'd first seen her climb out the boat. So she fit the witness statement. But what about motive?

Because her tea shop on the promenade and not the high street, Lacey had completely overlooked her when she'd been thinking of all the business Buck financially screwed over. Brooke's tearoom wasn't exactly high end, but she was a new business just establishing, and Lacey herself knew how every penny counted. She'd even admitted that Buck's payment had been suspended.

But maybe it wasn't money at all? Brooke and Buck had had an altercation at the auction. Brooke had seemed really wound up as she'd squared up to Buck. She'd even explained after that it reminded her of her violent ex. Had the experience made her feel threatened enough that she went for a row and ended up on the island, the very same place Buck ended up venturing to later? She'd be strong enough to kill him, with her wrestler's biceps, and blond enough to be mistaken for Daisy by Xavier when he saw her rowing back to shore.

Then there was the very simple fact that she was here. That Lacey's plan was to lure a killer to the island with the rumor of fake evidence, and Brooke had turned up.

Lacey didn't want to believe it, but her heartbeat was starting to increase. Brooke fit on the Venn diagram more neatly than anyone else had so far.

The bag, she reminded herself. Brooke didn't have a pink bag! Not only was pink not her style, but her own bag was right there in the corner of the tent, a dark black rucksack.

But even as she thought it, she felt a nagging doubt in the back of her mind

"Well?" Brooke asked, more insistently. "What evidence did you find?"

Lacey made a snap decision not to tell Brooke it was a lure. If Brooke was the killer, and thought Lacey knew something, she'd only reveal it if she thought she'd been trapped. If she learned that there was no evidence and that it was a lure, then the pressure would reduce and she wouldn't confess.

"It was Chester who found it," Lacey began. "He loves exploring the island. And digging. And he especially loves the ruins. Have you had a chance to see them yet?"

She was attempting to divert the conversation, to gather more information.

"The medieval castle?" Brooke said, the tenseness in her voice audible under what sounded like forced calmness. "Yes, I've seen it."

"You have? So you've visited before? When did you get the chance, you've only been here a few days?" Lacey chuckled, to keep up the pretense they were having a friendly conversation.

"The day of the auction," Brooke said, but her sentence cut off abruptly and her head darted up. She locked eyes with Lacey, and the look in them told her that she knew she'd said too much.

"Brooke," Lacey said, her heart feeling heavy. "Did you kill Buck?"

"No!" Brooke exclaimed. "I . . . It was . . . It wasn't like that!"

Tears shone in her eyes suddenly.

"What was it like?" Lacey asked, as softly as possible. She was treading very dangerous ground right now. She was on an abandoned island with no way off. "Tell me what happened. I'm your friend, Brooke, I'll understand."

"You saw what he was like!" Brooke cried. "He was a brute. A bully. I didn't . . . I didn't plan it!"

"I'm sure you didn't," Lacey said. Her voice had taken on the air of a school counselor, or a midwife dealing with a woman in the most painful throes of labor. "What did he do? Did he hurt you?"

"You saw him with the steak, didn't you? How furious he was about the dog. The hygiene. He said he'd get the health inspectors on me. He was black-mailing me. When I saw him at the auction arguing with you, I just flipped, you know? He reminded me so much of my ex. Afterwards, I came for a row, to calm down, and ended up here. I thought I was alone, that it was an island, I had no idea about the sandbar. So when he just suddenly appeared, I lost it. At first I thought he was a vision or something. A PTSD flashback. He was shouting at me, carrying on the fight from your store. There was no one else around, just the two of us. I started panicking. I thought he was going to hurt me. He kept going on and on about how he had money, and how I'd undermined him. He kept jabbing this wad of cash in my face. He pulled the bag out of its plastic carrier, and said, 'I just bought my wife this expensive handbag, I wouldn't have been able to do that if I didn't have money, would I?' It sort of hit me against my face and that's when I snapped. It was all instinct." She looked at Lacey. "I just grabbed the bag and tugged. He went flying forward, and hit the sand really hard. Then I got on his back and pushed him down and held him there until the fight was over. That's all I was doing. I was wrestling him. Except, when I got up, he was dead."

Lacey listened quietly, her heart slamming into her rib cage. No wonder Brooke had been so freaked out during their telephone conversation. Lacey had more or less described the altercation exactly, only assuming it was between Buck and Daisy, not Buck and Brooke. And no wonder she'd called the police during Lacey and Xavier's meeting. She'd in all likelihood known that Lacey would get arrested too, but decided it was collateral damage. She'd probably let go of Chester on purpose, hoping he'd run off and distract Lacey from working it out. All along, Brooke had been trying to steer Lacey away from the truth. All those moments Lacey thought they'd been bonding and becoming friends had just been about Brooke manipulating her.

Lacey stared at the woman she'd once considered a friend, as she carried on explaining.

"I was dazed. I didn't know what to do. I realized my fingerprints would be on the bag, so I filled it with rocks and threw it into the sea. The plastic bag Buck had pulled it from fluttered into the trees, but I'd not touched that so I left it."

Lacey thought of the moment the police officers had become so animated at the tree line. They must've found Buck's empty store bag.

"I didn't realize the strap had ripped off," Brooke said. "When you turned up at the tearoom with Superintendent Turner and put the strap on the table, I thought I was done for. But then he said the evidence was damaged because you didn't have gloves. I thought I'd gotten away with it."

"You blamed Taryn," Lacey said, recalling how Brooke had diverted the suspicions toward the boutique owner while they'd been talking.

"It wasn't my bag. I thought if you and the police thought the pink bag belonged to the killer, then you could trace it back to the store and see that I wasn't one of the customers who bought it. That I'd never even been in the boutique. I thought it would get me off the hook."

"And the sextant?" Lacey asked. "Was that you as well?"

Brooke looked ashamed. "I'm staying at Carol's. I can't afford my own place yet."

"So you went in Buck's room?"

"I passed it. The door was open. Housekeeping. They knew he and Daisy ate late, so decided to clean it then when he was out. He'd been making a nuisance. Slapping their asses and stuff. No one wants to do the shift but obviously the two would complain if not. So they did it then. I went past, the door was open and the sextant was just there. It felt like, I don't know, fate? Like my chance at retribution. My chance to put right the wrong of killing him. So I took it, for you. I was going to leave it in your greenhouse, but when I went into the garden I saw your back door was open, so I put it inside instead."

Lacey felt squeamish. Brooke was still acting like her friend, but Lacey knew their friendship was over. She couldn't be friends with a killer. Especially one who tried to justify their actions by blaming the victim. No matter how awful Buck was, no one deserved to die that way.

Brooke looked at her with appealing eyes. "Will you keep my secret, Lacey?"

"There's an innocent man sitting in jail right now because of you."

"I know. And if I could get Xavier out I would. But I can't go to prison, Lacey. I spent my whole life in the prison of an abusive marriage. I've only just gotten free. I can't."

"It's the right thing to do. The only way to make amends. You killed a man, and another will get blamed for it if you don't do the right thing now. Don't ruin any more lives. We'll get you a good lawyer. Tom's mom is one. You can argue self-defense, PTSD trigger."

"Lacey, that won't work!" Brooke wailed. "This isn't TV. In the real world there is no justice. All anyone will see is a woman who killed a man. It's a classic he said, she said. And we all know who jurors believe. I could have the best lawyer in the world and I'd still go down for this."

"If you don't hand yourself in, I'll do it for you," Lacey said. "I have to. I'll be charged for perverting the course of justice otherwise."

Brooke let out a long, deep sigh. For a moment, Lacey thought it was a sigh of resignation. Of acceptance. For a brief moment, she thought she'd talked the woman into handing herself in to the cops.

That was, until Brooke raised her head slowly up and said, "I was really hoping it wouldn't come to this."

She lunged for her rucksack, as lightning quick speed, and Lacey finally saw the single item she'd carried with her to the island. It was a knife.

CHAPTER TWENTY FIVE

Everything turned to slow motion. The knife came arcing toward Lacey, and she dodged, falling to her side. The knife sliced through the space she'd previously occupied, cutting a huge gash into the side of the tent. Wind whipped in through the opening, making the tent shake violently. Lacey dove for the gap, slinking through it, with Chester slipping out after her.

Out in the pouring rain, Lacey scrambled to her feet against the slippery sand. She raced straight ahead, not knowing where she was going, just knowing she had to get away. She glanced back briefly over her shoulder briefly in time to see the dark shape of Brooke emerging from the tent, looming up like a ghoul. The knife flashed in the moonlight.

I've got to call the police, Lacey thought as she ran, but at the same moment she was hit by the horrible realization that she'd left her cell in the tent.

"Chester, what are we going to do?" she squeaked.

Chester barked and started heading in a different direction. He was leading her somewhere. Lacey followed.

Before long, the ruins of the castle came into view. Lacey ran for them, heading inside in the hope of finding somewhere to hide. It was like being in a maze of crumbled rocks. The rain lashed through from above, because the roof had long since rotted away.

Lacey saw a set of stone steps and headed for them, wedging herself under the stone steps, in the shadows they cast. She brought her knees up to her chest.

Now what? she thought desperately. *I can't sit here for hours waiting for the sandbar to come back.*

Then she remembered the boat. Brooke had rowed here, and tied her boat up to the jetty, opposite the tent! If Lacey could make it back to the tent, she could grab her cell, then jump onto the boat and row away.

But before she had a chance to put her plan in action, she heard the sound of footsteps scudding against the stone floor. Brooke had found the ruins.

Lacey's breath stuck in her lungs. Was her hiding place good enough? Or would Brooke, knowing she had all the time in the world, thoroughly search the ruins for her?

"Lacey, I know you're in here," Brooke called. "Just, come out and let's talk alright?"

Talk? The time for talking was over long ago!

"I'll tell the police what I did, if that's what you really want," Brooke continued.

Her voice sounded strange in the echoing ruins, with the rain pattering in the background. Lacey could get a grasp on where she was in relation to her, but it felt close. The hairs on her arm were starting to stand on end.

"Come on, Lacey. We're friends. We can talk this out. Put it behind us."

Lacey knew it was a trick. Brooke was trying to play to her sympathies, just as she had all along. And she did have sympathy for her, still. If only she'd had proper counseling and treatment for her experiences, none of this would have happened. She might not have been triggered by Buck, or flashed back to the past.

Just then, Lacey heard the scuff of shoes on stone coming from far too close for comfort, and she bolted out from her hiding place and scurried up the steps. When she reached the top, she found most of the floor had given way, and in its place was a huge gaping hole that dropped down about twenty feet. Only a very narrow pathway linked this side of the staircase with the other side.

Lacey put her hand against the wall to guide her, finding it slippery from rain. Then she took a very careful step onto the ledge.

Suddenly, Lacey felt something give way underfoot. The stone was starting to crumble! She slipped, her fingertips grasping hold of the ridges in the stone.

Chester couldn't help himself. At the sight of his owner in dire straits, he barked.

Lacey steadied herself and began to inch back the way she'd come, toward the top of the staircase. She felt sweat dripping down her brow.

Then Brooke appeared at the bottom of the steps. Lacey saw her eyes assessing the situation, evaluating what to do, trying to work out if Lacey was going to die anyway in an accidental fall and save her all that trouble. With the rain driving down she looked just like something from a horror movie.

172

Barely thinking, Lacey leapt. She sprung across the chasm in the floor and landed on her chest on the other side. Winded, she let out a groan, then rolled onto her back and heaved herself up to her feet. Chester leapt the gap after her, and the two headed for the other staircase, Lacey wincing as she hobbled.

From behind, she heard the angry growl of Brooke, and the thudding of footsteps as the woman went back down the way she'd come.

Lacey ran down the steps and bolted for the exit, back out onto the island.

I've got to make it back to the tent, she thought.

She looked around for Chester and saw him anxiously looking behind at the castle ruins.

"Chester!" Lacey said, getting his attention. "We have to go to the tent. The tent."

He gave her an attentive look, then bolted off for the trees.

Lacey followed, diving into the relative shelter of the trees. Branches snagged at her, the little sharp pains like needles adding to the dull ache coming from her ribs. She must've bashed them badly when she'd landed on her chest. Hopefully nothing was broken.

The sound of rain on the canopy above was deafening. Beside her, a bedraggled-looking Chester had a very determined look on his face. Lacey put all her faith in him.

Before long, they reached the edge of the trees. Lacey peered out, seeing the tent ahead of her. She surveyed the area, looking for any signs of Brooke. But there were none. They must have lost her.

Lacey went for it, pounding across the to the tent and ducking in through the tear. She scrambled around, searching for her cell.

"There!" she cried, as she finally found it.

She turned, ready to jump back out the gap and run for the rowboat. But Brooke was right there.

"Thought I'd find you here," Brooke said through the tear in the tent. "Although I'm pretty sure that won't be of much use."

She was looking at the cell phone, and Lacey realized what she meant. There was no signal on the island.

"I really didn't want it to come to this," Brooke said, putting one foot through the gap. "I really wanted us to be mates."

She inched half of her body inside the tent. And that's when Chester struck.

He jumped, grabbing Brooke's arm in his jaws. The woman screamed and Lacey pulled open the zipper of the tent door and bolted out. She ran, heading toward the shoreline, even though it was completely exposed with nowhere to hide, not looking back out of fear of what might have happened to her savior dog.

She started running along the shoreline, searching for the jetty and rowboat. As she went, she kept dialing 999, but every time the call didn't connect. There was no reception on the island. The phone was useless.

Feeling desolate and hopeless, Lacey suddenly saw lights, coming from the sea. Flashlights?

Then a dark shape emerged from the sea onto the beach. It was the police dinghy! Superintendent Turner and DCI Lewis leapt out, guns drawn, and a whole load of officers came with them.

"Where's the perp?" Superintendent asked her.

Lacey turned and pointed at the tent. "It's Brooke."

"Is she armed?" DCI Lewis asked.

"She has a knife."

The detectives nodded and made hand gestures to the officers, then the whole group moved stealthy across the beach toward the tent.

Lacey could hardly believe it. She was safe. The cops were here. It was over.

Except for Chester . . .

She felt her legs go weak. Then, as she began to fall, strong arms grabbed her. She looked up and found herself staring into the eyes of Tom.

"What are you doing here?" she gasped.

"I came for you," he said. "Taryn told me what you were planning. I called the police right away, then rowed out here."

"It's Brooke," Lacey told him. "Brooke's the killer."

He held her tightly, shushing her and soothing her distress.

"Chester," Lacey managed to say, and then the tears started in earnest.

All at once, a lot of shouting came from the direction of the tent. Still wrapped in Tom's arms, Lacey turned her face toward it. The police came out, marching Brooke between them.

Then, emerging behind them, came Chester.

Lacey's heart soared. She heaved herself out of Tom's embrace and the dog came running down the beach toward her, tail wagging. She opened her arms and he leapt into them, putting his paws onto her shoulders.

Only now, with Chester safe and unharmed, could Lacey accept she was safe.

She watched, filled with sadness, as Brooke was cuffed. The woman bowed her head as she was marched toward the police dinghy.

It was over.

CHAPTER TWENTY SIX

"Thanks," Lacey said, accepting the plastic cup of vending machine hot chocolate from Tom.

He sank into the seat beside the hospital bed she was perched upon. The papery blue curtains were closed around her to give her some privacy, but she still felt very awkward sitting there soaked to the bone and shivering, wrapped in yet another one of those silver paramedics blankets. She looked like she'd been through some terrible trauma. Then she realized, she actually had.

She looked over at Tom, slumped, exhausted in the seat. He'd saved her, but she was filled with conflicting emotions. Perhaps it was the effects of the painkillers the ambulance staff had given her, but Lacey felt very bold.

"I saw you with another woman," she said.

Tom's expression turned to shock. "What?"

"Don't play dumb," Lacey told him. "I saw you having breakfast with a brunette."

His face transformed in an instant. "Oh!" Then he started to chuckle. "Oh, Lacey, you didn't think . . ." He shook his head, and inched up off the chair to kiss her forehead. "I was interviewing," he said, one hand on the side of her head. "For an assistant. I need more time. Time with you."

"Really?"

"Yes. Really! If you'd walked past an hour later you'd've seen me having breakfast with an overweight bald man."

"Oh," Lacey said, feeling foolish for having so quickly jumped to conclusions. "Why didn't you tell me you were hiring?"

Tom shrugged. "I guess it was going to be a surprise. I was planning on going to the focaccia course and then have her start the week after, show her the ropes, then take you away for a staycation."

176

"So you hired the brunette?" Lacey asked, feeling a small pang of insecurity to know Tom would be spending his long working days with a young woman. She could just imagine them giggling away as they made marzipan ferrets. "Not the overweight bald man."

For the first time in their relationship, Tom seemed to have picked up on her sub-text. He chuckled, and stroked her cheek tenderly.

"She was the best person for the job," he said, gently. "But I haven't offered her it yet. If you don't want me to, I won't."

Once again, the painkillers gave Lacey courage. "I guess I'm a little wary. Because I don't actually know you that well. I don't know whether I can trust you yet. It's not your fault. It's the fact that I trusted David for fourteen years and then he betrayed me. It's just going to take me awhile to be comfortable in a relationship again."

Tom nodded. He looked a little disappointed, but he did seem to understand. "We can take things as slow as you need," he said, softly, sitting back in his seat beside her. "There is something I should tell you though. Something I've been keeping to myself."

Lacey felt her heart begin to race immediately. "What is it?"

"My ex got back in touch. She asked to meet. She said she wants to reconcile." He tipped his head toward the ceiling, almost as if searching for divine inspiration.

"What did you say?"

"I said no, obviously."

Lacey hitched her knees up to her chest, hugging them. "David asked me to come home."

Tom tipped his head back down and their eyes met. "What did *you* say?"

Lacey gave a small shrug. "I said I'd think about it."

Just then, the curtain was pulled back and a nurse came in, her presence acting like a punctuation mark dumped in the middle of the awkward conversation. It was the same bubbly woman who'd met Lacey with the ambulance in A&E, where the police had immediately sent her once they'd returned to Wilfordshire, the one who'd drawn Lacey's blood, and given her a shot for tetanus, and put dressing on the scratches she'd acquired from the forest.

"Your bloods came back fine," the young nurse said, smiling kindly. She had a nice accent, the same one Lacey always heard on those sepia tinted ads that sold bread and Bakewell tarts. "And your heart, lungs, everything is okay. Blood pressure back to normal."

"No shock?" Tom asked from his seat.

"No shock," the nurse confirmed. "No concussion." She looked back to Lacey. "So we're happy to discharge you, if you feel ready to go."

Lacey nodded with relief. She was beyond ready to go. She was desperate to be back home, curled up on the couch with Chester and a nice cup of tea.

Lacey swung her legs over the side of the tall hospital bed, and leapt down.

"That's the best thing you could've told me," she said to the nurse, and thanks to her doped up state lowering her inhibitions, she pulled her into a hug. "You've been wonderful. You fixed me like some kind of magician."

The nurse chuckled. "It's my pleasure. But once the drugs wear off, you will be a little sore." She looked over at Tom. "Take care of her, won't you?"

Tom gave the nurse a smile, but it did not reach his eyes.

"I will," he said, his tone a little sad. "If she wants me to."

Lacey and Tom were silent the whole taxi ride back to Crag Cottage. Lacey didn't know how to restart the conversation they'd been having earlier, and with her painkillers starting to wear off, the reality of what they'd been talking about began to hit home. She should've just lied about what she'd said to David. Now she'd made everything awkward.

Gina was standing in the doorway when the cab pulled up to the cottage. Chester and Boudica came bounding across the lawn to greet Lacey, jumping up with their paws while she was still only halfway out the back seat.

"Quick, get inside, you!" Gina yelled. "I've made a fire, and the pizza delivery is on its way!"

Lacey laughed and looked over at Tom. "So much for homemade pizza, huh? I guess you'll have to make do with takeout."

"You want me to stay?"

She reached for him, taking his hand. "Of course I do, Tom."

A small smile played across his lips. "Okay. I'll stay. But you have *got* to stop calling it takeout! It's *takeaway*."

"Ew, no. I'll keep my Americanism, thank you very much."

They laughed, and Tom slung an arm around her shoulder, helping her to wobble up the garden path and in through the front door.

CHAPTER TWENTY SEVEN

The couch had just gotten to that comfy, molded to your body-shape, and the meat lover's pizza had filled Lacey's belly. With Chester dozing with his head in her lap, and Gina was snoring, and Tom laughing at the TV, Lacey felt like everything was all right in the world.

There was a knock at the door.

In her armchair, Gina snorted and woke with a start.

Lacey looked at Tom. "I bet that's Karl, coming to question me."

Tom stood. "I'll tell him you're concussed and you won't be ready for an interview until tomorrow."

Lacey smiled. "Thanks."

He left the room, and returned a moment later. Not with Superintendent Turner, but with Xavier.

Lacey was immediately embarrassed by her disheveled state, not to mention how much of a slob she looked with half eaten pizza boxes lying around the place. She attempted to sit up, but winced as her scrapes and bruises made themselves known.

"Please, stay seated," Xavier said, in his gentle Spanish accent.

"What are you doing here?" Lacey asked.

"I came to thank you," Xavier said. "And your dog. Because of you both, the police have dropped my charges. I am allowed to fly home now. I wanted to say goodbye before I left."

Lacey couldn't help but feel a little sad about the fact that Xavier was leaving. He seemed like a nice man. And he was a link to her father, even if only tenuously.

"It's been quite eventful," Lacey said.

"You could say that again," Xavier replied, chuckling.

Just then, another knock came at the door.

"Okay *that* will be Superintendent Turner," Lacey said.

Tom went to answer it.

"Blimey!" Gina said. "It's about to turn into a proper soiree in here!"

"Don't worry," Lacey said with a chuckle. "Tom's going to tell them I have a concussion!"

But when Tom returned, moments later, DCI Lewis and Superintendent Turner were right behind him. Lacey let out a groan.

"Can I please just have one evening to myself before I answer your questions?" she said with exasperation, looking from one officer to the next.

"Actually, that's not why we're here," DCI Lewis said. "We came to return this."

She placed a padlock and key on the coffee table, next to the open pizza box.

Gina leaned forward, peering at the padlock. "Is that—?"

"—it's the lock to my store!" Lacey exclaimed with sudden excitement. "Does that mean I can open up again tomorrow?"

DCI Lewis nodded, handing Lacey some paperwork that explained her property had been returned to her.

"Hey, wait a second," Lacey said, blinking at the paper. "It says here you're returning the items of mine that were taken into evidence. Did you take stuff out of my store? Do you have any idea how rare some of that stuff is?"

But her words were cut out by Superintendent Turner placing something on the other side of the pizza box. The sextant!

"I think you'll find that this is what the paperwork was referring to," he said.

Lacey couldn't believe it. She never thought she'd see it again.

"There were only partial fingerprint profiles on it," Superintendent Turner explained. "And far too many for it to be of any use. But we have more than enough other evidence to charge Brooke without it now anyway, thanks to you. So it's yours."

Lacey stared at the sextant, bewildered and delighted.

"But wait," she said, with sudden dawning. "Isn't it rightfully Daisy's? Brooke stole it from her hotel room, after all."

"She said she didn't want it," DCI Lewis said.

Lacey remembered the tearful widow's explanation in the tearooms, about how she'd been trying to get Buck to snap out of his delusional spending by demanding the most expensive, useless item she could.

"And anyway," DCI Lewis added, "the money never exchanged hands."

"And, if I recall, Buck refused to sign the certificate of ownership," Tom added.

Lacey leaned forward and picked up the sextant, shocked that it was back in her possession. She gazed at the object that had seen so many things, and lived so many lives.

Then she looked over at Xavier.

"It's yours."

"What?" the man said.

Lacey held it out, nudging it toward him. "It has sentimental value to you. It should be yours. Free of charge, of course."

Xavier shook his head. "I will not hear of it. Wasn't the money going to charity? Let me make a donation, at least."

"If you insist," Lacey said. "And if you really want to repay me, you could tell me everything you remember about your meeting with my father."

"Of course," he said, grinning from ear to ear with delight.

He picked up the sextant, and his dark chocolate eyes sparked with wonder.

Lacey sunk back against the couch, satisfied and grateful. It had all worked out in the end.

Epilogue

Lacey's plan to open up the store the following day didn't quite come to fruition. It took her two days of recuperation before she was physically able to return.

She arrived with Tom on one arm, and Chester beside her. Her ribs were still very bruised, so Tom opened the shutters for her, but she took control of unlocking the front door.

The dust stirred as she went inside, Tom and Chester following.

There were some signs of the police activity. Smudges on the walls. Scuffs on the floor from boots traipsing through. But beyond that, it was her usual store again. It felt like home.

"Are you sure you don't want me to say?" Tom asked for the thousandth time that morning.

She shook her head. "You have your own store to run. Louise isn't trained enough yet to be left there on her own." She took him in her arms and pressed a deep kiss onto his lips. "I promise you, I'll be fine."

"See you for Elevenses?" he asked.

"An al—"

"—mond croissant with apricot jam," he finished for her. He tapped his head. "I've got your order locked down."

She smiled and watched Tom leave.

Alone in her store, Lacey took a long deep breath. It would probably take a while before any customers came back, since they'd gotten used to it being closed. She decided to busy herself sweeping up the debris from where the police had been traipsing through.

While she was out in the backroom—where she discovered they'd drunk their way through her entire stash of tea—Lacey heard the bell tinkle. She was surprised, and headed out to the main store. A whole bunch of people had entered, and were perusing her shelves. Lacey felt her heart leap with glee.

She slipped straight back into friendly store clerk mode, feeling the routine like a comfort blanket around her. It felt so good to be back in the saddle once again.

Just then, Lacey noticed Taryn enter. For the first time ever, Lacey didn't let out a mental groan at the sight of her. Taryn had played her part in the whole plan beautifully and she had to give her credit for that.

"Oh good, it's picked back up in here," Taryn said, looking around at the handful of customers milling about the place.

Lacey wasn't sure what she was insinuating. Knowing Taryn, it wouldn't be something good.

"You can thank me," the boutique owner continued, looking smug. "I mean, I *have* been telling everyone about Brooke, so that they know you had nothing to do with Buck's murder."

"You have?" Lacey asked. Of course Taryn loved to gossip, but doing so to clear Lacey's name didn't seem her style.

"I can't risk some other store moving in here," the woman explained. "Not after my experience with Buck and Daisy. Turns out you're not the worst kind of American. It could be far worse. Better the devil you know. Ta-ta."

She turned on her heel and waltzed out. Lacey rolled her eyes. Same old Taryn.

Then the door opened again, and this time, in came a familiar face. It was the old man who'd bought the ballerina statue the day before her auction. And this time, he wasn't alone. He was with a woman and a child—the same woman and child Lacey had scared away the day she'd found the sextant back in her store.

"Hello," Lacey exclaimed, surprised to see them all together. "What brings you back here?"

"This is my daughter," the old man announced. "And granddaughter. I told them about the story about the ballerina figurine. They said they'd come in to look but were hassled out. So I thought they must've gotten a different clerk, because the one who served me was ever so nice and generous."

Lacey blushed. "Actually, it was me who served them that day." She looked at the woman and child. "I'm really very sorry about what happened that day. I was in a bit of a panic, and under a lot of stress."

The woman nodded, as if cautiously accepting Lacey's apology. The little girl tugged her sleeve.

"Can I get a ballerina now, Mummy?"

"Yes, darling. Let's go and look."

They went off toward the figurines, leaving Lacey with the elderly man.

"I'm sorry to hear you were going through a tough time," the man said, kindly. "May I ask, is everything okay now?"

Lacey looked across at Tom in his patisserie. And at Chester, in his usual spot sleeping in front of the counter. Then she looked back at the elderly gentleman and smiled.

"Everything's perfect."

Now Available for Pre-Order!

CRIME IN THE CAFÉ
(A Lacey Doyle Cozy Mystery—Book 3)

CRIME IN THE CAFE (A LACEY DOYLE COZY MYSTERY—BOOK 3) is book three in a charming new cozy mystery series by Fiona Grace.

Lacey Doyle, 39 years old and freshly divorced, has made a drastic change: she has walked away from the fast life of New York City and settled down in the quaint English seaside town of Wilfordshire.

Summer is nearly here, and Lacey has fallen more in love with the town and with her chef boyfriend. She has even made a best friend: the new owner of a local B&B. And when her friend needs her services for the decoration of her inn, buying nearly everything in Lacey's antique shop, her business even gets an extra boost.

Everything's going perfectly—until someone mysteriously dies in her friend's new B&B.

Their village turned upside down and her new friend's livelihood now in jeopardy, it's up to Lacey and her dog to get to the bottom of the mystery.

Book #4 in the series will be available soon!

CRIME IN THE CAFÉ
(A Lacey Doyle Cozy Mystery—Book 3)

Made in the USA
Las Vegas, NV
13 March 2024

87155723R00114